MW00629770

HOW I CONQUERED YOUR PLANET

John Swartzwelder

Kennydale Books
Chatsworth, California

Published by:
Kennydale Books
P.O. Box 3925
Chatsworth, California 91313-3925

First Printing March, 2006
Second Printing October, 2008

ISBN 13 (paperback edition) 978-0-9755799-4-7
ISBN 13 (hardback edition) 978-0-9755799-5-4
ISBN (paperback edition) 0-9755799-4-0
ISBN (hardback edition) 0-9755799-5-9

Library of Congress Control Number: 2006901140

Printed in the United States of America

CHAPTER ONE

First of all, it's not true that I led the Martian attack on Earth. I was in Battle Cruiser Number Four. So let's get that straight. I don't know how these things get started. Secondly, I can explain.

It all began innocently enough about a year and a half ago. I was chasing a criminal through the streets of Central City, honking at him to give himself up. I had spotted him breaking into the National Guard Armory and had taken off after him. He was on foot. I was driving a city bus.

It's pretty tough trying to run down a criminal at night, but it's even tougher when all of your passengers are screaming so loud you can't hear yourself think.

"Hey, stop all that praying back there!" I told them. "Can't you see I'm trying to drive? You! Sit down and quit trying to squirm through that window."

"I've got to get out!" He wailed frantically. "I've got to get out!"

"Sit down when the bus is in motion," I told him, pointing to the sign that said that. He reluctantly sat down. I frowned at him. "You better learn how to ride a bus, buddy."

I finally cornered the criminal, and about forty innocent bystanders, in the lobby of the Midtown Hotel. I was trying to decide whether to get out and handcuff him or just run over him with the bus, when he suddenly rolled up into a ball and disappeared in a puff of confetti. I hadn't expected that. He had fooled me. I picked up the biggest piece of confetti, which had his mocking smile on it, and put it in my pocket. I figured if there was a reward for this guy, maybe I could get part of it. His smile had to be worth something.

I turned the bus around in the lobby as best I could, gave the hotel people a false bus company name, told my passengers to quit throwing up or I would give them something to throw up about, and headed back out onto the street to continue my route.

I probably shouldn't have taken the time to go after that criminal. I had a schedule to keep. But I needed any extra money I could get. And I figured 9:40 pm is pretty much the same as 5:05 pm. It isn't, I guess, but what the hell is everybody yelling about? That's what I wanted to know.

What you probably want to know is: why is Frank Burly, the famous detective you've heard so much about, driving a city bus? The reason is, I had to take a second job to bring in some extra money, because my detective business hadn't been doing so well lately. After four years of serving the detective-hiring public, the detective-hiring public had caught on to me to a certain extent. Maybe Lincoln could fool everybody all the time, but I couldn't.

Unfortunately, my bus driving job hadn't been going too well either. Hey, can't I do anything right?

Once I got the bus out of the lobby and back on the road, all my passengers started criticizing the way I had been driving. Everybody's an expert. The kids in the back gave me the worst time. There's something about being in the back that brings out the worst in people. They were really making fun of me, and getting some pretty good laughs at my expense.

I hollered over my shoulder, with growing anger, that if they didn't quit being so funny at my expense, if they didn't start making their humor more generic, I was going to pull over to the side of the road, make everybody walk home, call everybody's parents, blow the damn bus up, and set fire to the world.

This chilly prospect didn't bother the kids, who thought it was a lot more interesting evening than they had planned, but it greatly alarmed some of the older passengers, who started trying to get off the bus again, even though we were going over 50 mph. I had to tilt the bus up on its side wheels to get them to slide back more or less into their seats. Then I had to deal with all the fake injuries, and spend ten or fifteen minutes saying soothing things like "snap out of it" and "you're not hurt" and "please, God, don't let him die" until everybody on the bus had calmed down again. These are the kinds of things bus drivers have to deal with.

Things quieted down after that, and nothing much more happened, except for a few wrecks, until I pulled into the last – and strangest – stop on my route; that new bus stop out by the crop circles. It hadn't been there a couple of weeks before, and there was this weird green glow around it all the time. But it was a bus stop and I was a bus, so I stopped. No one ever got off at this stop but there was always a small group of passengers waiting to board there, all asking to be taken to "nearest Earth city". "That would be Central City," I would tell them.

They all paid their fares with what looked like crops at first, but after they had handed them to me I could see they were dollar bills. After we got going again I would notice that the fare box was all gummed up with crops now, but by then I couldn't remember whose fare was whose, so I had to just forget it and turn the crops in with the other money. Let the bookkeeping guys at the depot figure it out. They're paid to do it. I've got a bus to drive.

On this particular night, one of the passengers waiting at the Crop Circle Stop had forgotten to bring his fare and was taking a lot of ribbing from his friends about it. Mounting the steps into the bus he said "Hubbit hubbit hah!" and pulled a dollar out of my ass and paid his fare with that. For the rest of the trip I had to yell at the passengers to leave my rear end alone. There wasn't any more money in there. And if there was, it was mine.

Back at the depot, after my shift was over, I found that the guys had filled my locker with paste again and were behind a pile of boxes laughing as I tried to open the door, then quickly tried to close it again. They loved their little practical jokes, damn them. So I was in an extra bad mood when Mr. Thorson called me into his office.

I entered Mr. Thorson's office with my pants filled with paste and my hat smoking from another joke.

"How'd the shift go tonight, Burly?"

"Fine, Mr. Thorson."

"How many accidents this time?"

"Four."

"Better. But not good enough."

"Huh?"

He started chewing me out, reminding me of all the things I had done wrong since I joined the firm. The fiery crashes, the speeding tickets, those missing busses I couldn't account for. All the usual stuff.

I nodded off during part of this recitation, which didn't improve his humor.

"Are you asleep, Burly?"

He had to ask this several times before I answered.

"No, of course not," I said sleepily, rubbing

my eyes and yawning. "What kind of an employee do you think I am?"

"That is precisely what we are discussing."

"Good. It's about time."

"And now there's this 'money' you've been collecting for fares. Money that is nothing more than garbage." He held up a money bag with a dollar sign on it and ears of corn sticking out of it. "Explain this, Burly."

"Well sir, I have a theory about that."

"I'd like to hear it."

"Yes sir. First of all, I think we're going about this in the wrong way blaming me for it. I think we can rule me out right from the start. It's those guys out at that new bus stop by the crop circles. The passengers who get on there. They're to blame."

At this, Mr. Thorson's chief accountant, a small gremlin-like man, whose name, appropriately enough, was Arthur Gremlin, looked up from his work and stared at me. Gremlin had been the driving force behind putting in the new bus stop out by the crop circles. At first the company had felt it was a waste of good bus stop sign material, but Gremlin had been proven right by the constant flow of passengers who boarded busses there. He was immediately given a raise, and, to show that bus companies can be as progressive and forward thinking as the next form of transportation, stops were put in in all the cornfields in the state. The Crop Circle Stop was Arthur Gremlin's baby, so when he went back to his work he kept one eye and both ears on the conversation that was going on.

"How are our passengers to blame?" asked Mr. Thorson.

"The people who get on the bus at that stop are magicians or wizards or something, Mr. Thorson," I said. "They can turn corn into money. At least for awhile. And that's not all that's weird about them. They also have feelers."

"Feelers!"

"Yes sir. Mr. Thorson. Alien feelers. Under their hats. Which brings me to my theory. I think the Earth is being invaded by Magicians From The Moon. They're invading us and riding our busses."

"The Moon!"

"Or maybe the Van Allen Radiation Belts. I'm not completely sure what part of space they're from at this point. Check back with me later on that."

He looked at me like I was nuts. "I'm looking at you like you're nuts", he said.

Arthur Gremlin was looking at me funny too. I looked back at him even funnier, and that stopped that. I guess we know who can look the funniest now. He looked away.

Now that I'd come out with my theory, actually put it into so many words, I was starting to wonder if there was anything to it. It made sense to me, I was willing to stake my reputation, if any, on it, but I was well aware that throughout the course of my life I'd almost never been right about anything. You've got to take stats like that into account. You can't ignore inside information like that. So suddenly I wasn't so sure of myself.

Mr. Thorson was looking at me with that mixture of contempt and pity I know so well. "I understand making mistakes on the job and trying to cover them up, Burly. I'm not always perfect at my job either..."

"You can say that again!" I agreed enthusiastically. It always pays to butter up the boss. "Of all the bumbling, half-witted..."

"But there's one part of my job I am good at. And that's firing people. You're fired!" he said powerfully.

For a moment I was too stunned to speak. Then I started going to sleep again. Then I got mad. "Hey, if I'd known you were going to fire me I wouldn't have stood here and let you chew me out like this. I would have shown more backbone."

"Yes, well, you didn't. So get out!"

"Yes, Mr. Thorson. Wait a minute, I mean, screw you, Mr. Thorson."

I went down to payroll to collect my final paycheck. They gave me a plastic bag full of garbage. They said it was my share of what I'd been bringing in for the company. Was it all there? I looked at the ears of corn and thumbed through some of them.

"Yeah, I guess it's all here."

I cleaned out my locker, at least as much as I was going to clean it – screw 'em, screw everybody around here – then I said goodbye to my bus company friends.

"What's your name again? Eugene? Goodbye forever, Eugene. I will miss you horribly. The time we had together... hey, come back when I'm talking to you."

I waved to the others as I walked through the depot for the last time. "See ya Stretch, Curly, Pimple Face, Cross-Eye, Dribble-Mouth."

I went out, pausing at the door to take one last look at the old place. Not to fix it in my memory, just to see if I could erase it completely from my mind. As I was looking at it, I saw my giggling "friends" peeking out from behind a half-closed door and realized I was about to be the victim of one last practical joke. Sure enough, when I got to the parking lot, I saw that they had blown up my car.

CHAPTER TWO

"Frank Burly Investigations. No, Mr. Burly isn't here right now. Probably sleeping it off somewhere... uh huh... but you don't want him anyway. He's a lousy detective... no, worse than them... I know it doesn't seem possible, but.... Hey, listen mister, I used to work for the Three Stooges, and I'm telling you this guy is worse... You want my advice? Hire a good detective. The good ones don't cost any more." She hung up the phone and looked at me.

I shook my head. "I'm afraid you won't do."

I had been auditioning new secretaries. This one, I felt, was too honest. She disagreed.

"My mother taught me that honesty was the best policy."

"Your mother's fired too."

I really couldn't afford a secretary anyway. As I mentioned before, my money situation wasn't all that great. And now that I'd lost my second income, things were even worse. I'd originally thought this was going to be a real bang-up year, so I had spent a lot of money upgrading the office and installing a Disneyland style line to slowly wind clients up to my desk. That cost me over eight thousand dollars because I had the guys from Disney put it in for me. If you're going to do something, I figured at the time, you should do it right. I've since realized if you're going to do something, you should do it as half-assed as you can. It's cheaper, faster, easier, and nobody in this world or the next can tell the difference. Nobody can. Check it out.

All my normal day to day expenses were going up too. The price of a private investigator's license had suddenly jumped up by 50% to help pay for some stupid school children's lunches. The government thought a bunch of little kids' lunches were more important than my lunch. That's bureaucratic thinking for you. I could write a book about bureaucratic thinking. Or maybe a play would be better. It might make a better play.

Even my rent had gone up during the year. My landlord couldn't justify the increase by pointing to the inflation rate, which was quite low at the time, so he just said that my office had gotten $50 better, it was $50 closer to the ocean or something. I told him that $50 was a lot of money. I pointed out that, for example, I could have him killed for $50. He said he could have me killed for $50 too. By the same guy. We stared at each other for awhile, fingering our wallets, then I decided to pay the additional rent.

The only thing that wasn't going up was the daily rate I charged my clients. I couldn't raise that because it was felt by everybody that I was already charging more than I was worth. Can't argue with everybody, I guess. Everybody can't be wrong.

The problem was I wasn't very good at things. Everybody knows somebody like that. And I was the guy I knew. I wasn't very dependable either. And I guess I didn't smell too good most of the time. I didn't have much going for me, to be honest.

Sometimes I wished there were an easier planet to live on because this one was so hard for me. I realized there was no place like home. I mean, there couldn't be two places this bad. But that didn't make me like it any better.

During the year I had tried all kinds of creative ways to increase my business. I offered volume discounts to victims of more than one crime, and began accepting Crime Stamps.

My radio campaign didn't generate much business, though I never saw what was wrong with it. The commercial went like this:

ME: (HIGH VOICE) "What's the matter, Edna?"

ME: (MIDDLE VOICE) "My detective isn't solving my cases lately."

ME: (HIGH VOICE) "Sounds like you need to hire Frank Burly."

ME (MIDDLE VOICE) "That's what I was thinking."

It had the right message. Maybe the

"boinnnngggg!" sounds I put in after each couple of words hurt the tone.

I tried holding a "One Second Sale". If you had your first crime solved* in the regular amount of time, you got your second crime solved* in one second.

The Frank Burly Double Your Money Back Detective School didn't work out. Most of the people who signed up for it weren't serious about learning about detecting. They were just in it for the Double Your Money Back. They got their money, all right. If that's all they cared about, fine. But I gave each of them a failing grade.

When I couldn't bring any more cash in, I tried to lower the amount going out. I switched to smaller caliber bullets, started making my own clothes, and finding my own gas. And I tried to find a secretary who would answer the phone for tips.

The applicants who showed up weren't acceptable. Either they were too honest, too clumsy (I've still got a telephone receiver in my back somewhere), or they didn't understand how a phone worked and would just sit there and listen to it ring until we both started to die.

On this particular day, there were about a dozen applicants for the job waiting in my waiting room, but I didn't hold out much hope for them. Still, I had to find somebody. I was thinking it might be a good time to lower my standards. I spent a few minutes with a pencil and a piece of paper figuring out how low my standards could go. I decided I would now accept minorities, cripples and the criminally insane. One-eyed men were back in the running, as well as people without voice boxes. I reduced the minimum number of arms, legs and teeth I would accept. And I decided they no longer had to speak English. They could communicate with me in the language of their choice. I figured with low standards like that, just about everybody would be able to work for me.

I flipped the switch on my solid gold intercom (another expense!) and called in the next applicant. But that person turned out to be gone. So were the next three applicants. In fact, everyone in my waiting room was gone except for one small gremliny-looking man, who I instantly recognized as Arthur Gremlin, the bookkeeper for Mr. Thorson, down at the bus company. I said it was a small world and he said he thought so too.

"Small. And weak."

I asked what he was doing here and he said he had quit the bus company when he heard about the great job I was offering. I admitted the job wasn't that great – my full page ads in the newspaper had exaggerated the benefits a little bit. For example there would be no chance for advancement. My company only had two jobs. He could never work his way up from his job to my job. He said that was all right. He would be satisfied to remain a secretary.

I asked where the other applicants had gone,

the ones who had been here ahead of him, and would have probably gotten the job before he did, and he said the answer to that was simple. There were no other applicants, and never had been. They simply never existed.

"Oh, good," I said. "I was hoping it was something simple like that. Come on in."

He followed me hissing into the office, then sat down opposite me at the desk and hissed. He had done a lot of hissing back at the bus company too, I remembered.

"Hey, what's with all the hissing?"

He drew back and hissed, but didn't explain. I didn't bring the subject up again, but I think he did actually cut down a little bit on the hissing. I started going through my routine interview questions.

"Born?"

"Yes."

"Where?"

"Here."

"In my office? You're lying."

"No, on this planet."

"Oh. Well good, because that's a requirement." I made a mental note to make that a requirement.

It was obvious by the end of the interview that Arthur Gremlin was a gem. He satisfied all of my requirements for a secretary. He could type, open and close the door unaided, and answer the phone when it rang – not before, not long after, but when. But there was something weird about the guy. He kind of creeped me out. I also didn't like the thoughts he kept trying to put in my head. Thoughts of hiring him, and trusting him. As good as he was, I decided I'd better keep looking.

I put on as sorrowful a face as I could and shook my head. "I'm sorry, but you've got the job."

He smiled.

"That is to say, you're hired. For life. With a big fat raise."

He bowed his head slightly in gratitude.

I reassembled my thoughts, took a deep breath and said: "You have excellent qualifications but when can you start?"

He smiled again. "I already have."

CHAPTER THREE

Over the next few days I discovered that I had hired a surprisingly dedicated secretary, who listened in on my phone calls, patted down my visitors, looked through my desk for me each morning before I got in, even appeared in my dreams taking notes.

He seemed to be trying to get into the Secretary Hall Of Fame, if there was such a place. I didn't think there was, but I didn't tell him that. Better to let him have his dreams. But I did tell him I wasn't going to be raising his salary, if that was what he was thinking. If that's what all this good work was about. A deal is a deal. He said he wasn't in the secretarial game for the money. He had other reasons. Just the prestige, I guess.

My clients didn't like him. He scared them. They complained about his X-ray eyes. I thought they were exaggerating, but they showed me the X-rays, so I guess they weren't kidding. I told one of them he should be happy to find out about that broken bone, but he wasn't.

I have to admit he made me nervous sometimes too. But when I thought of firing him, a kind of electric shock went through my brain, and I started stuffing dirty socks in my mouth. So I stopped thinking about it.

Even with a brand new secretary parked out front, I was still finding it hard to get clients. Something always seemed to happen just before the money changed hands. One potential client was a theater owner who came into my office sucking his hand.

"Your secretary bit me!"

"Were you teasing him?"

"Well...sure, but..."

"You've got to expect that to happen then. You've only got yourself to blame."

He sucked his sore hand again, then sat down and told me what he had come about.

His story was a strange one and involved magicians, which made me think of the strange people I had picked up at that bus stop out by the crop circles. A small bolt of lightning that seemed to come from my secretary shot across the room and went through my brain. I stopped thinking about the bus stop and the lightning bolt went away. I guess there are some things we're just not meant to think about. Magicians and bus stops are the two I've noticed so far.

The man said he was the manager of the Palace Theater downtown. Last week the magician he had as his feature act had gone haywire somehow, hypnotized himself into thinking he was a chicken, and then started demanding corn from the audience.

The audience was amused at first, then began to grow frightened as his demands grew more vehement. When a few members of the audience actually gave him some corn he said it wasn't enough. Finally the audience fled.

The theater manager had instantly fired the magician, giving him the bum's rush out the front door and a hearty kick towards the future. As he was turning to go back into the theater he noticed a man dressed in magician's clothes leaning against a lamp post idly pulling rabbits out of a hat and dropping them in a waste receptacle designed for that purpose.

"Hey! Are you a magician?"

"I am."

Another rabbit was removed and disposed of.

"How'd you like to work for the Thunder Wonder Circus Brothers Show?"

"I accept your generous offer."

The theater manager paused in his story to mop both our brows. His story was an exciting one, though it was a little weak in the third act. But I didn't see where a job for me came in.

"Was he a fake or something? Is that your problem?"

"No, he's a magician all right. And a great one. He can pull a rabbit out of a hat without putting one in there first."

"So what's the problem?"

"He's ruining my business! Driving my customers away! He starts off his performances with a few normal tricks, then as soon as he has the audience's complete attention, he hypnotizes them and pumps them for military information."

"Does he get much?"

"Sure. Theater audiences know everything. So I tell him to stick to the standard tricks, they're good enough for Central City, but he says he won't change his act for anybody. I keep trying to fire the guy but every time I do I end up giving him a raise, a better parking place, and a box full of my stuff. I can't afford to fire him again. He's already making more than I am."

"What exactly do you want me to do?" I didn't know what he wanted me to do. "Perform on stage with him?" I hazarded. "Because I don't do that."

He looked at me like I was stupid. Why do people always look at me like that? "No," he said, "I want you to find out what kind of hold this guy has on me and my audiences, and how I can get rid of him. I'll pay you double your normal rate. Interested?"

I was interested all right. I needed the money. My rent was almost due and I knew better than to ask for an extension from my landlord, the appropriately named Mr. Asshole. (He pronounces it 'ah-SHOLEY', but no one else ever does.) So this job couldn't have come at a better time.

I noticed the Gremlin was watching to see what I would do. I opened my mouth to accept the assignment, then I noticed the theater manager was looking at me strangely.

"Why are you stapling your mouth closed?"

"Mphmknxks." I replied, stapling faster.

"Hey, I didn't come here to audition a mouth stapling act. Audiences don't like them. They don't understand them. I need a detective. Do you want the job or not?"

"Grmpkliglemorfl!"

He watched as I applied a final staple, and began methodically smearing glue on the lower half of my face, then said: "I guess I'll try one of the other detectives in the building."

I watched him go, disappointedly. "Fxup yak!" I hollered.

The Gremlin let the man out the door, sat back down at his desk and smiled at me. I didn't smile back. I wouldn't be doing any smiling for some time.

Arthur Gremlin was doing a lot of smiling these days. He had seemed pretty tense when he first joined the firm, but the more time he spent with me, and the more he saw me in action, the more he relaxed.

Finally after watching me spend three entire days trying to get a carton of milk open, he wiped the milk off his face and relaxed completely for the first time. It's like something that had been nagging at him finally went away.

The next day, after he had made a very long distance call that the phone company charged me $23,000 for, (more expenses!) my fortunes abruptly changed. All of a sudden I started getting a lot of new business. Enough so I actually got some use out of that Disneyland line I'd had installed in front of my desk. When I asked where these new clients had heard of me – was it my ad in the Daily Detective or my comical TV infomercial, the one where I play all the parts and speak in the Swedish accent? – they would exchange glances with the Gremlin and then say they guessed they had heard of me everywhere. That made me feel good. You can't get more famous than that.

And these weren't just routine cases I was suddenly getting. They were plum assignments that I could charge big money for. And my new clients seemed to be willing to pay whatever I asked. As an experiment, I tried asking for $1000 a day, plus expenses, plus more expenses, plus those first expenses again. They didn't even blink an eye. In fact, none of these new clients ever blinked their eyes. No eyelids. I told them if they wanted to get some lids for those eyes, I wasn't a doctor, but I would do my best. They declined. Fine, I said, I just wanted them to know that I was here to serve them.

Over the next couple of months I happily carried out a series of unusual assignments for these new clients. They seemed to be satisfied with my work, and I was more than satisfied with the way they paid their bills in cash. I'd already made my nut for the year and was working on next year.

One client wanted me to get back his copy of our nation's Air Defense Plans which his mother had given him ("The Case Of The Missing Defense Plans"). Another wondered where his maps of escape routes from the city went. ("The Case Of The Missing Escape Route Maps") Other clients had me measuring troop strength, planting explosives, sabotaging railroads, air terminals and power grids, and beating up atomic scientists.

As the weeks went by, I gradually began to notice that the jobs I'd been doing for these clients were a little offbeat. I hadn't questioned the assignments at first, because I needed the money and it doesn't pay to argue with someone who is writing you a check. If you do, they might not finish writing that check.

But when I found myself about to shoot the Mayor in the back of the head for some client I suddenly thought: Wait a minute! What am I doing?

I seemed to be acting like a crook. And doing a crooked thing. That didn't sound like me. I'm a good man. Something strange was going on. And since I was a part of it, I needed to find out what it was. I decided that what I needed was a detective to look into this. And since I am, to the best of my knowledge, the cheapest detective in history, I decided to hire me.

CHAPTER FOUR

I wasn't sure who I could trust at this point. I wasn't even sure I could trust my own secretary. So I did my investigating late at night, during lunch hours and so on. Each time I ducked out of the office, I would make a different excuse to the Gremlin, saying I had to get another driver's license – the one I had gotten yesterday was only a one-day one – or I had to get my teeth rotated, or my nose cleaned, or I had to go outside because it was too inside in here. I don't think he suspected anything at first, because I have this reputation for being kind of stupid. A reputation like that comes in handy sometimes. Most of the time it ruins everything, but sometimes it's handy.

I started my investigations by looking into who these people were who had been hiring me. Surprisingly, all of them turned out to be professional magicians. And they all lived in the same building. What are the odds of that?

Then I took a closer look at the jobs they'd been having me do for them. Now that these jobs were finished, now that I wasn't being blinded by a paycheck, I could see I'd done a surprisingly large amount of damage all over town. The places I'd been sent to "investigate" were all either shut down now, or burned down, or being run by little men who looked something, but not exactly, like Arthur Gremlin. Come to think of it, my magician clients looked a lot like him too. This started to make me a little suspicious of Arthur Gremlin. And vice versa.

The Gremlin first started getting suspicious of me when he saw me reading letters I had removed from a secret drawer in his desk with a crowbar and a small amount of explosives. The letters were written in an alien tongue. Even the punctuation looked kind of scary. But I couldn't decipher them. The Gremlin frowned when he saw me reading them, but seemed to accept my explanation that I had tripped on the rug and cushioned my fall by ripping open his desk and reading his letters.

Our mutual suspicion increased when an Air Force General came to see me. Someone had sabotaged his missile base. The police couldn't figure out who did it, and he wasn't too keen about telling Washington about it. He was hoping I might be able to solve the mystery, since that was my business.

I started to tell him that he'd come to the right place, because I had sabotaged his missile base. But before I could get nine words out, I found myself stuffing his military decorations and good conduct medals into my mouth. He frowned at this and asked what the meaning of it was. Then, when I started eating his uniform, he took his business elsewhere.

The Gremlin and I looked at each other. Neither one of us was smiling. Both of us hissed.

I continued my investigations, but I was no longer doing it alone. I would make my excuse of the day and slip out, but as I walked the street I noticed I was being shadowed – mostly by real shadows, but there would always be one shadow that didn't stop exactly when I stopped and started up again a little after I started. And it smoked a cigarette when I wasn't smoking one. And it got ahead of me sometimes and had to wait for me to catch up.

Each day the atmosphere became a little more tense around the office. Now when I made a lame excuse and ducked out of work, the Gremlin also made a lame excuse – often the same one – and we went down the elevator together. Once we got down to street level we split up, but pretty soon I noticed I was being tailed again. And it wasn't just the Gremlin who was watching me now. It seemed like everyone was watching me.

Magicians would turn their heads to look at me – sometimes in the middle of performances. Sometimes they even went so far as to make me think I was a chicken. And, looking back on it, I'm not sure I wasn't a chicken. Those eggs in my refrigerator came from somewhere. You explain it.

Other times as I drove down the street I could have sworn I was being tailed by a space ship.

It was an uncomfortable position for a detective to be in. The people I'd been tailing had started tailing me. That happens a lot in my business though. You get used to it, even though you never exactly like it. You've got to learn to laugh at yourself, as long as everyone else is doing it. Otherwise you'll be the only person who isn't laughing.

Then the day came that I knew had to come sometime. The day I'd feared above all others. The day I couldn't think of an excuse to leave the office. I couldn't even think of the excuses I'd used before, so I couldn't say I was going to do that one again. My mind was a blank.

I thought alcohol might help me think – that's what it's for, after all – so I opened a bottle and started drinking, while I tried to come up with an idea. I couldn't think of anything at first, but partway through the second bottle I started thinking what a good buddy of mine Arthur Gremlin was. What a pal. The little knucklehead. Then I started thinking that he and I should fight. Then I wished I could see him again, but knew I never could. Then I remembered I was supposed to be thinking of an excuse to get away from him. I got back to work on that, but before I'd gotten very far, the Gremlin abruptly put on his coat and hat, made an excuse I wished I had thought of, and left. I was stunned. Now I didn't need to think of an excuse at all! I could investigate anything I wanted undisturbed. I wondered why.

I trailed the Gremlin to a magic shop in the theater district that catered mostly to professional magicians. I stayed back and watched for awhile from across the street, but he didn't come back out. Finally I walked over to the shop. It was closed for a "private party", a sign on the door said. There were skulls and crossbones on this sign.

I opened the door and went inside. There was no party that I could see. Everything was dark and quiet. That didn't necessarily mean it wasn't a party. I'd had parties like that. But where was Arthur Gremlin? I started to switch on the lights and the radio, but checked myself at the last moment. Better stay inconspicuous, Burly, I thought.

Due to the darkness, I stumbled over a number of things as I made my way stealthily through the shop. I knocked over magic tricks, stage props, costumes, and the cash register. I accidentally made myself disappear for awhile, nearly sawed myself in half, and had a knock-down-drag-out fight with a rabbit-lined hat.

The racket caused someone in the back room to open the door and look into the shop. He didn't see anything amiss, though one of the marionettes hanging from the ceiling was unusually large and sweaty.

He peered at it for a long moment, frowned when it hiccupped, peered at it a little longer, then closed the door. The magic shop was dark again.

I got down, removed as many strings from myself as I could, and began creeping towards the door to the back room.

I tried to look through the keyhole, but this was one of those doors that didn't have one. So I tried to make a keyhole, very very quietly, using a very small chisel and a very quiet hammer.

After ten minutes of this, I wasn't making much progress so I got a bigger chisel and the King Of The Hammers, and went back to work. Suddenly the door opened again and the same person looked out. I froze with my chisel raised and a demented expression on my face. The man looked past me into the shop for a few moments, then closed the door again.

I was getting a little frustrated. I wanted very much to know what was going on in that back room, but there didn't seem to be any stealthy way to do it. So, finally I just opened the door and walked in.

"Sorry I'm late guys," I said, pretending I knew everybody. "You would not believe the traffic on Made-Up Avenue today. So what are we doing? What's the meeting about? Jesus!"

The room was full of strange people dressed as Martians and making "beep beep" sounds.

Maps on the walls showed Martian armies advancing in all directions, stabbing and death-raying Earthmen, and laying waste to the countryside. Washington D.C. and Central City had X's drawn through them and scary flags flying over them. Insert ovals on the maps showed pictures of smiling Martian Generals giving us the thumbs up. Some of the Martians portrayed on the maps were eating dead Earthmen's bodies, but were being chastised by their comrades for doing so.

Everyone turned to look at me. The beeps in the room took on a more ominous tone. I figured it was time to leave.

"Is this Yankee Stadium?" I bluffed. "No? I'll try upstairs then. It's probably upstairs."

I backed slowly out of the room and through the magic shop again, banging into the same things I had banged into coming in. Then I banged into Arthur Gremlin, who was blocking the way out of the shop, holding a large gun.

I stopped. The back room emptied out and the strange men began coming towards me, beeping louder.

I tried another bluff. "I think he went that way," I told them, pointing at a blank wall. "I suggest we spread out. You two take the North Side. You three, Chinatown. Mugsy... where's Mugsy?"

I looked around the room, supposedly to see if I could spot Mugsy, but actually to see if this was working. It wasn't. They kept coming towards me.

I made one last attempt to fool them. "Look behind you," I said sharply. No one turned. "Hey, come on, look behind you." A few turned this time, but not enough. I shook my head. "All of you have to look for this to work."

One of the men took a bottle of something

down from a shelf and opened it, then held it out to me.

"Drink this," he said.

"What is it, doc?"

"Medicine."

"Good, because I'm not feeling very well right now."

I drank it.

CHAPTER FIVE

I woke up in a shooting gallery. I was revolving slowly through the target area, then back behind the backdrop, then past the targets again. Pellets were bouncing off of me. As I revolved past the carnie each time I said: "Uh... excuse me... ", but then I was gone again.

I couldn't remember anything. I couldn't remember how I'd gotten there. I couldn't remember what the prize was for knocking me over. I couldn't even remember who I was.

The second question was answered soon enough. The next time I came around, everybody decided to let fly at me at the same time. I went over. It cost the carnie almost all of the prizes on the second shelf. And it cost me my position.

The next thing I knew I was in the back of the shooting gallery, upside down in a garbage can.

I extricated myself and started wandering around aimlessly, wondering who I was. I assumed I wasn't a very important man.

Otherwise I wouldn't have been used by the carnival as a shooting gallery target. All I had in my pockets were a comb, a couple of clues, and some stuff I stole from the carnival.

The carnie had no information to offer that might help unravel the mystery. Some people had driven up and offered him a free target. That was all he knew about it.

I left the carnival grounds and began walking the streets, looking for some clue as to my identity. I didn't see any statues of me, or see my face on any stamps, and nobody was bowing down to me, so that reinforced my theory that I wasn't that important.

I must have stopped at every Information Booth in town, but none of them had any information about me. I wondered how those places managed to stay in business.

At one point I wandered through a factory which seemed to have been built just to endanger me. There were giant saw blades, pounding mallets, huge drills, and mechanical arms that tried to pull me to pieces when I went by them on the conveyor belt. I nearly got killed in there. I wondered what that factory was trying to make. I never did find out.

Finally, as I was heading back to the carnival to see if I could get my old target job back, I ran into some people who knew me! It was a group of teenage kids. They said my name was Frank Burly. I liked it. It was a good solid descriptive name for a frank and burly guy like me, I felt. I asked them what I did for a living, and they said I was their servant.

A couple of weeks later, while I was scrubbing the floors for the young masters, the doorbell rang.

"Junior Purple Gang Headquarters," I told the visitors efficiently. "May I ask who's calling?"

It was a young man and woman who seemed to know me: Dottie and Chuck Steak.

"Frank Burly!" shrieked Dottie. "What are you doing here? Why are you wearing that butler's uniform?"

I explained that I had always worked here. I had always worn this uniform. I had been born into slavery to these fine young men.

Instead of saying "Oh, that explains that then." Or "Oh, yeah, that's right. Now we remember." Dottie and Chuck both looked accusingly at the young masters who had just entered the room.

One of them looked a little ashamed when he was confronted with what he had done, but the others looked defiant, or just laughed.

My new friends told me I was a well known detective, not a servant, and escorted me back to my office.

When I arrived, the Gremlin was sitting at what I was told was my desk, talking on my phone, and wearing one of my suits. He quickly resumed his position at his secretarial desk and watched me curiously.

So now I was back where I was supposed to be, but I still couldn't remember what I was supposed to do.

My friends knew what to do, because they had seen it on every TV show ever filmed. A sharp blow, or brutal clout, to the head with some sort of blunt instrument was what was needed to bring back my memory. That's the real danger of television you never read about. Teaching people crap like that.

Over the next week, they hit my head with everything from ball peen hammers to television sets. Anything that would raise a lump. They even tried hitting me with a product that was specially designed for hitting people on the head that they saw on TV for $19.95. Unfortunately, it fell apart after the first hit, but they did get a free Tongue Yanker with their order.

To everybody's surprise, none of these medical treatments worked. I was starting to remember a few things, but the memories all had to do with being hit on the head.

But friends never give up. Not when there's still something left they can hit you with.

Finally, when they had started backing different kinds of cars over my head, to see if one of those would work, my brain, in an obvious attempt at self-preservation, started remembering things. In a rush, it all came back to me. I remembered my misspent youth, my misspent middle age, and the time I was misspending now. I also remembered the meeting I had blundered into – the one with the space aliens and the maps.

This was important information. It had to be reported to the police.

I thanked my hard-working friends, ducked a few final sledge-hammer blows and started for the police station. The Gremlin closed up his desk and followed me.

"I wish to report that we're being overrun by aliens from another planet," I told two bored detectives.

"Is that so? Which planet?"

"Uh..."

"C'mon, we haven't got all day."

"Don't you work here all day?"

"Wise guy, eh? What's that got to do with it?" He turned to his partner. "Wise guy. Asking us if we work here all day. Thinks that means we've got all the time in the world."

"Wise guys are like that, chief. He's got a point though, hasn't he chief? We do have to be here all day, whether he hurries up or not. All day tomorrow too."

"In theory, yes, but..."

I broke into this discussion impatiently. "Our entire military industrial complex is being compromised."

"By who?"

"Well... by me, actually. But I'm not the ringleader. I'm just a stooge."

I described all the things I'd been doing for my clients. The cops' eyes narrowed.

"How did they get you to do these awful things you said you have done?"

"Well, they paid me handsomely."

"Is that all someone has to do to get you to break the law? Pay you?"

"Well, that's the first thing they have to do. There might be some other stipulations. Working conditions and so on."

Then I started telling them about Arthur Gremlin and the strange things I'd seen at the meeting in the magic shop. But before I could get very far into my story, I found myself stuffing billy clubs and police badges into my mouth. Then my mouth snapped closed and appeared to slowly zip itself shut. I yanked part of my mouth open and tried to keep talking, but my mouth kept biting my hand and threatening me.

The cops watched with that kind of deadpan watchful look cops have, as I rolled around on the floor, fighting with my own mouth. Finally I hit my mouth hard enough to disable it and it just hung there loosely. But I couldn't talk anymore. Nobody wanted me to anyway. We'd all had enough.

The Gremlin was outside the police station, watching me as I came out, pulling police equipment out of my mouth. He didn't look happy. I didn't care. I wasn't happy either. Neither were the cops. Nobody was happy today.

As I walked home, with my mouth muttering apologies I wouldn't listen to, I saw a sign shaped like an arrow. It was pointing to a door. Written on the arrow was the word "Clues". Of course a detective can't pass up clues. Clues are gold. Even if you can't use them yourself, you can always trade them to other detectives or send them in to Detective's Weekly for a chance to win a prize. A box of sea monkeys or something. I checked to make sure there wasn't a sign that said "Trap", then opened the door and walked in.

The moment I got into the room, the door slammed shut and was bolted from the outside.

I tried to get it open, but it wouldn't budge. I looked around the room. It was filled with people seated in rows facing a stewardess. I recognized some of them. Former clients of mine. "Hiya Merko, Professor Future."

They looked up at me, then went back to their in-flight magazines.

Suddenly the room shuddered and began to rise into the air making outer-spacey sounds and emitting sparks.

Then the captain came over the intercom saying there would be no smoking until we had reached our cruising altitude. This was Flight 723 to Mars.

CHAPTER SIX

As the space ship roared up through the stratosphere, I tried repeatedly to get off. There had been a mistake, I felt. I wasn't supposed to be in the stratosphere. I was a ground kind of guy. I was asked several times by the stewardess to sit down and quit opening the door, as I had caused several passengers to be sucked out into the void. I told her I seemed to have gotten on to a flying saucer somehow. No harm done, but when could I get off? She informed me this was a nonstop flight. We'd be landing on Mars in a week.

That was not acceptable to me, I told her. I wanted this vessel turned around, and I wanted it turned around now. If it wasn't turned around now, there would be big trouble.

Unfortunately, we were beyond the Earth's gravity by this point, and it's hard to threaten people when you're bobbing around in front of them, sometimes upside down, sometimes sideways, and nearby passengers are kind of playing with you, batting you back and forth across the aisle to each other, and keeping a running score of who's ahead.

"You're laughing now," I told the stewardess, sternly, "Laughing so hard you can hardly see straight, but you won't be laughing for long."

The passengers played with me for a little while longer, then grew tired of me and batted me back towards my seat.

I sat there for awhile, fuming, then raised my hand with a question for the stewardess. "Does the pilot of this vessel carry a weapon of any kind?"

"Yes," said the stewardess.

I put down my hand. There went my kill-everybody-and-run idea.

Since threats weren't getting me anywhere, I tried bribery. But neither the stewardess nor any other member of the flight crew would accept money for not doing their jobs. Finally I accepted the stewardess' $20 bill to sit down and shut up for the rest of the voyage. Am I the only one who takes bribes anymore?

For the next seven days I killed time as best as I could, trying to read their magazines, watching the in-flight movies – some of which featured has-been American actors along with the mostly Martian cast – and trying to get more money from the stewardess for all the sitting down and shutting up I was doing for her. I said the $20 she had given me wasn't enough. I needed more now. She said she didn't have any more.

On the seventh day, I could see a red planet

out of my window. It was Mars, all right. Okay, that does it, I thought. I've got to get out of here.

I got out of my seat, crossed to the hatch and started yanking on it. It took several members of the flight crew, and several more $20 bills, to get me back to my seat.

"I've got to get out of here," I explained, reasonably, to anyone who would listen.

They said everybody would be getting out of here in a few minutes. Just be patient.

Sure enough, the saucer's speed began to slow dramatically, and we began our descent into the Martian atmosphere. Fortunately for me, I was pretty ignorant about science. Otherwise I would have been worried about the lack of oxygen, the freezing temperatures, the harmful cosmic rays, the low atmospheric pressure, the wildly elliptical orbit, and all that other stuff. I didn't know planets could be different like that. A scientist would have been scared. Me, I didn't give a shit.

And I was right not to worry, as it turned out. Once we had landed and I had gotten off the saucer, I noticed things didn't seem all that different here. The elliptical orbit bothered me a little bit at first, but that's all.

I tried to breeze through security at the terminal, like all the other passengers were doing, but there was a problem with my identification papers – the problem being that I didn't have any. They asked me for my passport. I didn't have a passport. Then they asked me for my official Martian ID card. I told them I didn't eat that kind of cereal. More security people gathered around me.

"Do you have an Interplanetary Travel Permit?" one of them asked.

"I might. What does it look like?"

"If you had one you would know what it looked like."

"I think you might be overestimating my intelligence," I said stiffly.

I said they were welcome to look through my wallet, but then I noticed they were already doing that.

They asked me to turn myself inside out, so they could compare my insides to some kind of list they had. I said I couldn't. Couldn't or wouldn't? Well, both, I guess. They didn't like my attitude. I didn't like their attitude either. It was a standoff.

They huddled for awhile, then told me I was going to have to wait in an Official Waiting Area – which turned out to be a chair – until such time as I had proper papers. I asked how I was going to get these proper papers sitting in the chair and they said that was no longer their problem. It was the chair's problem now.

I didn't want any trouble – at least not any more than I already had – so I sat down in the chair. Sitting in the chair next to me was a skeleton. After a couple of hours, I tried sitting in a different chair, one that seemed more promising, to have more going for it, to see if that would result in more action. It didn't.

Since nobody seemed to be paying much attention to me, (I was the chair's problem, not theirs) I got up and wandered out into the main concourse. I heard lots of sirens going off as I left the security area, but nobody followed me right away because they were too busy holding their hands over their ears and trying to turn the sirens down. I found out later they'd been having problems with that ever since they had built that terminal.

As I passed through each security checkpoint, more sirens went off and more people began holding their ears and making phone calls to the siren company.

I wandered outside and took a look around. I wondered why I was brought to this planet, and what I was supposed to do now? Certainly not just walk up and down the streets eating a hot dog like I was currently doing. No one would have brought me millions of miles through space just for that. Nobody's that eccentric. I asked a few pedestrians what they thought was going on, but they just gave me a look and hurried away. Of course I hadn't shaved or bathed in a week – five weeks, come to think of it. That might have had something to do with it.

The only people I met who weren't afraid to talk to me were people who wanted to sell me things. They didn't seem to be interested in the fact that I didn't want the things they were selling, or that I was a monster from another planet. All that mattered to them was making sure I didn't miss out on a great bargain.

"It's one of a kind," they would say, waving something awful in my face.

"Good."

"You'll never see another one," they would add, making it squeak and smile.

"I hope to God you're right."

Since nobody was giving me any information, and I'd already bought three of those squeaky smiley things, I finally decided to quit worrying about why I was here and just spend the day taking in the sights. Martian cities are something to see, let me tell you. There's neon and chrome everywhere, and electricity going up poles, and lots of theremin sounds. You could tell you were on Mars all right. It had all the flash and glitter of a drive-in movie theater. I could tell the Martians were far ahead of us. Or at least as far ahead of us as drive-in movie theaters are.

I had a small camera with me, so I started taking pictures of anything that looked interesting. It occurred to me that pictures of a Martian city might be worth money back on Earth. Assuming I ever got back to Earth, of course.

Finally I got tired of walking and stopped at an outdoor café. There was a newspaper on the chair next to me. It was an extra. All about the lunatic who had escaped from authorities at the terminal. I elbowed the guy at the next table and showed him the paper.

"Does this look like me?"

He looked at the picture, then at me.

"Kind of," he said. "Screw your face up a little more."

"What do you mean 'a little more'?"

"Never mind."

I wanted to know what he meant, but at that moment, a small man in some kind of official uniform rushed up to my table, mopping his forehead and looking apologetic.

"Frank Burly?"

"Speaking."

"Thank heavens I've found you. I was delayed in traffic or I would have met you at the spaceport. Come with me. You're under arrest."

Since he didn't have a badge or any weapon that I could see, I stayed seated. I don't get up just because somebody tells me to. I looked pointedly at his gun hand and cleared my throat. He apologized again and looked through his pockets until he found a ray gun. He pointed it at me and repeated his assertion that I was under arrest. I nodded and went along with him.

I was escorted to a nearby government building and turned over to a larger, less apologetic man.

"I bid you welcome to our world," he said. "Strip to your shorts."

I did as I was asked. My clothes were taken away, and I was given a kind of futuristic smock to wear. Then I was escorted into a small room where three stern-faced men sat glaring at me. I was certainly meeting a lot of men today. I sat down. No one said anything for awhile.

I decided it would be best to be pleasant, since these people, whoever they were, seemed to be holding all the cards. I smiled at them. "Hello," I said engagingly.

They stared at me.

"My name is Frank Burly."

Silence.

"Friendly Frank Burly, they call me. The Inquisitor's Friend."

More silence. I slicked back my hair and brushed some crumbs off my lap.

"I hope my appearance is pleasing to you. As well as my demeanor."

They continued to stare at me stonily. I started to get steamed. "Aw, who cares, anyway? So what? Who are you guys anyhow?"

"We are The Council," said the one in the middle, whose name was a Martian word that sounded a lot like Frederick.

"That's kind of vague, isn't it?" I asked. "I mean, 'The Council' doesn't really explain who you are."

"You see? He thinks so too," said the man on Frederick's left.

"Quiet, Philip," said Frederick. "We'll resume our discussion about that at 'The Arguing Time'."

"There's another one!" Philip and I both exclaimed.

"Silence!" snapped Frederick. "You were brought to Mars before 'The Council', Mr. Burly, because it was feared you were becoming a danger to our plans."

"What plans?"

"Never mind."

"I want to hear about those plans."

They wouldn't tell me any more.

"Well if I'm such a danger to these "plans" you claim to have but can't produce, why did you bother to bring me all the way up here? Why didn't you just kill me?"

"We never thought of that," said Philip. They looked at me with sudden respect. It's about time somebody looked at me with respect. A man needs that once in awhile.

The third member of The Council, a gaunt aged man with a long white beard, whose name sounded like it was "Stinky", held up the camera that had been found in my pants pocket.

"You have been taking photographs of our most top secret parks, statues, stray dogs and delivery trucks. With this..." He squinted his eyes to read the brand name. "SpyMaster 3000. Why should we not treat you as a spy?"

"Spies aren't the only people who take pictures. Saboteurs do it too. And perverts." I tried to think of other people who took pictures, but couldn't think of any more. "Everybody does it."

They didn't seem convinced. Stinky examined the Spymaster 3000 again, accidentally taking his own picture a hundred times.

I started to get impatient. "Hey, when can I get out of here? When can I go home?"

"When you have answered all of our questions," said Frederick.

"Okay, then, let's get on with it."

"Very well. What weapons does your planet have to attack us with?"

"Or to defend against us," added Philip.

"Quiet."

"Oh, yeah, right."

"Answer, Earthman."

"Earth doesn't have any weapons to attack you with. Earth thinks Mars is uninhabited."

Philip said: "But your movies..."

"Pure fiction."

"What!"

"Where do they think flying saucers come from then?" demanded Frederick.

"Most people think the Air Force is making all that flying saucer stuff up."

"Why?"

"Most people don't know."

The Council members wrote down this new information, after erasing a lot of their earlier notes.

"I see... and um... what about nuclear bombs?" asked Frederick. "How many nuclear bombs does the Earth have, Mr. Burly? Be honest now."

"Uh... seven."

The Council members exchanged meaningful looks.

Stinky shook his head. "Oh, Man! Man! Once long ago we too had our Atomic Age. We nearly destroyed ourselves. But we learned to control our emotions, we gained wisdom, and so the danger passed. But you, with your stupid minds, are not ready to wield such power."

"And you are, eh?"

"Never mind us. We're talking about you. You're not ready. We're plenty ready."

"Baloney."

Stinky bristled. "That's one of the things holding your planet back – smart remarks like that. Oh, Man! Man!"

I was getting mad. "I'm liable to sock you in the nose in a minute," I warned them. "Don't think it couldn't happen."

"You better not sock The Council in the nose," warned Frederick.

"That's out," added Philip.

"Okay, I won't. But watch your mouth."

"Agreed."

"Anyway," I explained, "our atomic bombs are for peaceful purposes."

"Such as?"

"Uh... blowing up... wars."

This set Stinky off again. "Oh, Man! Man!"

Frederick held up a restraining hand. Stinky sat back down.

"Now to the most important question," said Frederick. "How much do you know about our activities on Earth and how much have you told others?"

I told them the few things I knew, and some of the things I'd guessed. They listened attentively.

"Accurate as far as it goes," admitted Frederick. "Though I don't understand the part about the Van Allen Radiation Belts."

"That's just a theory at this point," I explained.

"I see... and who have you shared this information with?"

"I told the cops some of it, but they couldn't really understand what I was saying because my mouth was full of their stuff."

"You told no one else?"

"No."

They relaxed. "Then no harm has been done," said Philip. He indicated me. "What shall we do with him?"

"Let's return him home unharmed."

"We weren't talking to you, Mr. Burly."

They talked it over. They didn't see how they could return me to Earth with what I knew now. "He could tell them about The Council!" fretted Frederick.

I raised a hand. "This is a stupid question, but..."

"All your questions are stupid."

"Yes... well... anyway... since you're so advanced and everything, why can't you just remove my memories of the past week, then send me home? I won't know any of this ever happened. I'll be a week late for everything for the rest of my life, but what else is new?"

They were intrigued by the idea, with one modification. Why not wipe out my entire memory and replace it with something they liked better?

"Hey, wait a minute..." I said.

The Council voted. None of my votes were counted, because they said I wasn't a member of The Council. It was decided that I would be brainwashed and reprogrammed to be a Martian. My treatments would begin at once.

I needed to do something quick. I figured our germs might do them in, I'd read something about that somewhere, so I tried coughing in their faces. After about ten coughs they told me to quit it. I tried a couple more coughs, then gave it up.

Now that my fate had been decided, and we didn't have to worry about me anymore, the Martians became less formal and more chatty.

Philip asked me: "When you were on Earth did you ever see a television program called 'My Favorite Martian'?"

"Yeah. Stinks."

All three men looked stunned and hurt.

CHAPTER SEVEN

"Hello, Mr. Burly."

"Am I brainwashed yet?"

"No, we haven't even gotten your coat off yet. And I've only just now said hello."

"Because I'm hungry."

"There will be food breaks."

I thought about this. "Is this a food break?"

The brain specialist's smile was beginning to look a little forced. "No..."

"Because... okay, look, here's my problem... my metabolism is delicately balanced, like a racing car. And, like a racing car, if I don't get a sandwich..."

"Get him something to eat."

It was my first day at the hospital. They said they didn't know how long I was in for. They said it depended on how cooperative my brain was. I said my brain was very cooperative. It always cooperated. Because it wanted to get out of here. They said good.

While I was eating my sandwich, and explaining why I might need another (sometimes my body is like one racing car, sometimes two), I was introduced to the brainwashing team that had been assigned to my case. It was composed of Dr. Xpct, a doctor so experienced – who had washed so many brains – he just didn't care anymore. Because of this experience and attitude, he was chosen to head up the team. I told him that this was how we did things on Earth too and was glad to meet him and he told me to be silent.

The second member of the team was a young doctor who had never washed a brain before and was all youthful enthusiasm, always jumping around excitedly, yelling things like: "Let me wash his brain first! Is that his brain? Let me wash it!" He was valuable for the energy he brought to the team, and because he made everybody else feel smart.

The third and final member of the team was a tough looking doctor who just leaned against the wall in his bulging lab coat all day, staring at me with half-closed eyes, and flipping a small brain up in the air and catching it in his hand. He usually played the part of the "bad brainwasher" when they started in on their "good brainwasher/bad brainwasher" routine.

Now that I knew who they were, they sat me down and told me who I was. Who I was really.

"You're not an Earthman."

"I'm not."

"No, you're a Martian."

"Ah. Am I brainwashed now? That didn't take long. You guys are GOOD."

"We'll tell you when you're brainwashed," Dr. Xpct said. "Just relax and let us do our job." He turned to an assistant. "Open up his head."

It took them awhile to get into my head because I've got a lot of bone there. Nature didn't skimp when it came to my skull. Of course I'm tough all over. You've got to be when you piss people off all the time.

Once they had gotten the top of my head off, they found that instead of having two hemispheres, my brain was just one big block. And there was evidence that people had been there before them.

"Did you know you've been brainwashed before?"

"How would I know that?"

"Looks like it's been done dozens of times over the years. Looks like everybody's been doing it."

Several assistant brainwashers crowded around to look. "I can actually see my face in your brain," said one of them, impressed. "Hey, look Bob! See how funny I look in this guy's brain?"

His associate took a look. "You always look like that."

"I do not! Quit kidding."

The youngest member of the brainwashing team ran up past the two doctors who were now shoving each other playfully. "Hey let me see my face!"

They were all amazed at how highly my

brain had been polished by the repeated washings. "It's amazing there's any brain left at all," one of them said admiringly.

I felt the area of my head where my brain was. (Or 'wasn't' to hear them tell it). I'd heard people say things like that before, but I thought they were just insulting me. I didn't know they were doctors.

Since we were discussing my medical condition, I took the opportunity to point out my rear end. "Sometimes I find it hard to take a crap too. Maybe you can look into my butt when you're done with my head."

"No, we're strictly brain men. You'll have to see a butt doctor for that."

I wasn't happy about this. "Great. Now I've got to see two doctors."

I had to sign papers before the treatments began saying that I agreed to submit myself voluntarily to whatever treatments might pop into their heads, insisted that no precautions be taken, and actually wanted them to kill me. These releases protected them, they said, from any future legal problems arising from my case, or any feeling of responsibility or need to be careful. I tried to get them to sign something like that for me – so I'd be in the clear too – but they wouldn't do it.

Over the next few weeks, holding the releases I had signed in one hand and their scalpels in the other, they really let my brain have it. They hacked pieces off of it, flushed it with experimental serums, yelled information into it, and wrote facts on it with a felt tip pen.

They even took my brain out at one point and washed it with soap and water to see if that would do any good. I could have told them it wouldn't work, if I had had a brain.

I got plenty of good old fashioned electroshock therapy too. They surgically implanted a power cord into the back of my head and then plugged me into the wall, sometimes leaving me that way for hours when they were busy doing something else.

"What kind of lamp is that?" visitors to the facility would ask.

"Oh, that's not a lamp," the scientists would say, winking to each other.

"It's giving off a lot of light."

"Yes. But it's also thrashing around and pleading for somebody to help it. How many lamps do that?"

"Not many, I guess."

"Not many is right."

My treatment also included long chats with Dr. Xpct. He would tell me the real truth about myself – the things I should be remembering. And I would try my best to remember them. I wanted to help the process along as much as I could because I wanted to get this thing over with. I had to go to the bathroom for one thing. But it was hard for me to believe all of the things Dr. Xpct was saying. I found myself resisting.

"I am not a Martian! I am a human being!"

"Then where did you get those feelers?"

"Oh, yeah, I see what you mean. I get the

point you're making. Forget what I said about... hey, these feelers come off."

"Please leave the feelers alone, Mr. Burly."

"Yeah, but..."

"Leave them ALONE."

As my treatment progressed, I began to learn more and more about the wonderful life I had here on Mars, and how foolish I would be to throw it all away by remembering something different. They taught me about my family, my friends, and my many personal accomplishments. I had gotten straight A's in school, they told me. I was proud of that and wondered why I didn't remember it? And when I was nine they said I had won a small prize. At my insistence, they showed me this prize, which turned out to be a comb Dr. Xpct kept in his back pocket. I started liking this life I had up here. I had been kind of a loser on Earth. I could admit that now that it wasn't true.

Then I said, wait a minute, if I was a Martian and my life had been one success after another, why were they brainwashing me? Isn't brainwashing something you do to some kind of enemy? Maybe one from another planet? They said they'd get back to me on that. Well, you can't expect to learn everything in a day.

When I wasn't being brainwashed they kept me in a nice room on the first floor of the building and let me roam free on the grounds "wherever I wanted". I put that in quotes because if I tried to go outside the grounds, even an inch, the hospital dog would get me.

Despite my apparent confinement, Dr. Xpct said I wasn't a prisoner. In fact, I was an important member of the research community here. I was officially designated as "Number Six". Doctor Xpct, I noticed, was "Number Eight". "Get me some coffee, asshole," I said. He frowned, thought for a moment, then went to the closet and got himself a new number tag. Now he was "Number Four". I looked at our numbers, then asked him if he wanted some coffee. He said not right now.

They measured my progress each day on a large diagnostic machine which doubled as a punishment machine when I wasn't progressing fast enough, or when I mouthed off. It was less expensive and took up less space than having two machines, they told me. "Okay, I'll buy one," I said, starting to reach into my smock. But they said they weren't trying to sell me the machine, they were just telling me about it. I was glad to be corrected.

Finally they decided my brainwashing was complete enough. I was mostly brainwashed. This was good news. I wagged my vestigial tail when I heard this. But I was concerned about the "mostly" part. Let's finish this job, guys. Let's do it right. They said the government had other things to do. They couldn't just spend all their time brainwashing me. There was more to public service than that. They wouldn't get re-elected if all they did for the public was just brainwash me all day. That made sense to me. Anyway, "mostly" was pretty good. I was pretty sure I was a Martian now and that seemed to be as close as they could get. If they tried to get the last little bit, they told me, they started losing ground.

"The problem is, your brain doesn't retain much information."

"Tell me about it. That's the understatement of the year."

They looked pleased. They had come up with the understatement of the year! One of them confided to me later that this was the second year in a row they had won it.

Now that I was officially cured, I was free to go. They returned my clothes to me and sent me on my way, remembering at the last moment to give me back the top of my head.

As I walked out of the clinic, a peaceful and contented smile was on my face. It stayed on my face until the tape finally worked itself loose halfway home.

On the way home I passed the good old Grxxpxyx Brothers Theater. I remembered sneaking in there when I was a young Martian to see Gloria Tentacle pictures. Then I remembered not being sure I remembered that. Then I remembered being shocked and shocked and shocked. Then I remembered remembering again.

I turned into the driveway of my typical suburban Martian home. On the way up the walk I waved at my neighbor, Norton. He looked at me like he'd never seen me before. This turned out to be a running joke with him over the next few months. That Norton, always good for a laugh.

I noticed the backyard had a swing-set, which made me think I must have kids. I looked at the pictures in my wallet. Sure enough, kids all right. And I loved them deeply. I hoped these weren't the best pictures you could take of them, because they looked kind of like alligators to me.

I walked up to my house, opened the screen door and entered. "Honey!" I called. "I'm home!"

CHAPTER EIGHT

I was DoublePlusGlad to be home again at last. It had been so long, I'd almost forgotten what it was like.

My wife met me as I came through the door.

"Fix the sink!" she demanded.

"Yes...er...dearest," I said. Then I looked a little embarrassed. "I've forgotten your name, if I ever knew it."

"Is that all I mean to you?"

"Apparently."

She frowned.

"I mean, that's what it's beginning to look like," I said hastily.

She frowned more.

I fumbled to come up with an explanation for why I couldn't remember her name. "You must not be much of a wife."

Boy was that the wrong thing to say! Me and my big Martian mouth.

I tried to fix things by giving her a big kiss. She stiffened.

"What is the meaning of this gesture?"

"It's a kiss."

"No, I mean why are you kissing me on the back of the head?"

"Oh, is that the back of your head?"

"Yes."

"Sorry. Is this the front? Gosh you're beautiful."

Our relationship was getting off to a rocky start this time around, but I was confident we would be great pals again soon.

The kids didn't take to me right away either. I guess I'd been away too long.

"You're not my father!" said the shorter of my two boys, the one who looked most like an alligator.

"Well I wouldn't have thought so either," I said, patting what I hoped to God was his head. "I'm just going by what the cops said."

I took a look around the house. It seemed like a perfectly normal modest suburban home. The perfect thing for a perfectly normal modest suburban Martian like myself. The only thing ostentatious about it was the presence of hundreds of thousands of dollars worth of surveillance equipment and bugging devices all around the house, all pointed at me.

I repositioned a couple of them so whoever was watching me could see me better. No point in spending good money on machines like that if you don't use them.

Now that I knew that I was a Martian, I felt I should dress the part. No one had laughed at my clothes yet, at least not to my face, but when

I looked in the mirror, something in the back of my mind told me I didn't look like a Martian. That had to be remedied before I did anything else. I couldn't find any Martian clothes in any of the regular Martian clothing shops for some reason, so I finally had to get the bulk of my wardrobe from a costume shop. Bubble helmet, ray gun, spacesuit, etc. Everyone looked at me when I walked down the street in them so I knew I was dressed right. But my wife and kids were horrified, and insisted I go back to my regular clothes. Women! Kids!

The next morning I went back to work at my old job. I'd been away so long I had kind of forgotten what I was supposed to do. They reminded me that my position was "Earth Monitor". It sounded like an important job. And an easy one too. Because the Earth wasn't likely to move around much. I went to work with great enthusiasm. I like easy jobs. I'm good at those.

After I'd been monitoring for awhile, my supervisor came in and reminded me to concentrate my monitoring on military installations, rocket bases and nuclear testing sites. He said I could watch ball games anytime, and shouldn't be using expensive equipment for things like that. I was glad to be corrected.

Over the next few months I did my best to get used to living 150 million miles away. Surprisingly, it wasn't that hard.

Living on Mars isn't that much different from living on Earth. Their cars have bigger fins than ours do. And their music is a little weird. No matter what song is on, it always sounds like something is about to happen. And most places on Mars it's kind of hard to breath the air. (Something about "oxygen". There's no "oxygen" or something.) But the main difference, I guess, is the people you meet. They're Martians.

Martians look a lot like us, though they are slightly smaller and have somewhat insectoid features. They're sensitive about this, so you should be careful not to point it out, like I did when I snapped my fingers and said to my wife: "Now I know where I've seen your face before! On a grasshopper!" I was in the dog house for a week for that one.

The most noticeable difference between Martians and Earthmen is in the brain department. It isn't that Martians are smarter than Earthmen, (they're smarter than me, of course. Being 150 million miles farther away didn't make me any smarter than I was before. I mean, how could it?) but they do have mental abilities Earthmen don't possess. They can create illusions – make you think you are a barnyard animal for instance. And they can control your mind with theirs and make you do all kinds of crazy things. Like pick a card.

Practically everyone I met could easily take over my mind. Then they would use my great strength for their own purposes, like carrying sacks of things for them or giving their enemies a good sock in the "nose".

Sometimes two Martians would grab hold of my mind at the same time and jerk me backwards and forwards, towards one or the other, with my fists balled up in fury, with the stronger mind eventually winning, and the weaker mind getting a deserved pounding. If the Martians were pretty equally matched I often ended up spinning around in the center of the battleground, beating myself to pieces.

I asked them how they did their tricks. Was it Mars' yellow sun? They said no, it was mostly just getting people to look somewhere else.

Maybe it was because of the differences in our mental abilities, or maybe it was because I hadn't taken a shower all year, but I didn't make many friends on Mars. I tried to hang around with my old brainwashing buddies, but they had new friends now and didn't have time for me. I understood that. Life moves on. It was nothing to cry about. So after awhile I stopped crying.

My family life wasn't going too well either. I tried to be a good father, but I guess I wasn't too successful at it. I tried to teach my kids, Skrank and Scrudge, baseball and they bit me. I tried to teach them to respect their flag and country and they bit me again. I tried to hide behind a building under some tarps, and they found me and bit me. Where do kids pick up this stuff? In school? Maybe it's the schooling. I'm going to blame that.

My job as Earth monitor hadn't turned out to be as exciting as I thought it would be. Nothing much ever happened down there except ball games, and I wasn't allowed to watch those. I never saw any unusual troop movements or bomb tests or anything. There was the odd rocket launch, but it usually was just a global positioning satellite or something. Occasionally probes from Earth landed in one of our parks and roamed around until they flipped over and burned. Nobody paid much attention to them because there was no way to get them to look at you. Something about their programming I guess. Then one day I saw something through my monitoring equipment that was very unusual. And very important, I felt. I called my supervisor over.

"They're dismantling all their nuclear weapons! They're turning them into... it looks like... Love Beads!"

"Turning their nuclear weapons into Love Beads! Are you sure about this?"

"As sure as I've ever been about anything," I replied truthfully. "And John Astin is involved somehow."

"Good work, Burly."

"Thank you very much, Mr. Xplycx."

He rushed off to contact his superiors. I adjusted the eyepiece on my telescope and went back to my monitoring of what I later realized must have been a very bad drive-in movie. So I guess I'm at least partially responsible for what happened next.

Later that day, as I was driving home, I heard over the radio that April 30th – that was just a few months from now – would be "Earth Day".

Everyone in my neighborhood was very

excited that Earth Day was coming at last. I'd never heard of it myself, but I was sure it would be DoublePlusGreat.

My first thought was that Earth Day must be some kind of festival where everyone dresses up in costumes and pretends to be an Earthman. But I soon realized that I was wrong, unless everyone was planning on going to the party as a soldier. Just about everyone in town was out in the streets doing military style drilling, and practicing shooting strange looking guns at people who resembled me more than it did them. This made me a little nervous. Even though I was born right here in good old Mars City, I knew I wasn't built like a standard Martian. I was aware of my Earthy good looks. I hoped no one with poor eyesight and a gun would mistake me for an Earthman.

But I still didn't make the connection between shooting people who looked like Earthmen and "Earth Day". Then I found out that Earth Day was the day the attack on the Earth was to begin.

I was stunned. Attack the Earth? Of course I'd never been there, but it seemed like a decent enough place. What had they ever done to us? The Martian propaganda machine was ready with an answer to that question.

Posters immediately started appearing all over town that showed Earthmen thumbing their big noses at our beliefs, crapping noisily on our culture, and laughing when our women tripped over things. Radio programs dramatized these outrages and made them seem even worse now that we could actually hear all the crapping and laughing.

As I listened to all the Martian propaganda I got madder and madder. Those lousy Earthmen, I thought. Where do they get off treating us good old Martians like that? I went downtown and enlisted.

CHAPTER NINE

When I entered the induction center it was packed. It seemed like everybody wanted to personally teach those paper-hanging sons of bitches on Earth a lesson.

As I stood in line I saw some of the young Martians I had grown up with and waved to them, calling them by their boyhood nicknames.

"Hey Snapper! Remember all that time we spent together as kids? All the crazy things we did?"

"No."

"Neither do I. And yet those events happened. Remember our many mutual acquaintances?"

"No."

"Nope, me neither. Great times. Well, goodbye."

When I got to the front of the line, they had me fill out a lot of papers. It was easy to remember all my personal information and family history, because I'd just had all of that beaten into me by experts.

I passed the physical, but it took awhile. A lot of time was spent with the doctors yelling "Hey! Look at this!" They kept lowering big cameras down my throat to take pictures of what they found down there. Sometimes I wish I wasn't so interesting.

Before I was sworn in I had to swear obedience to the All-Powerful, Pretty-Much-All-Knowing, He's-Practically-Everywhere Martian God Zog.

"Uh... this is the first I've heard of this god," I said.

"Swear allegiance to him."

"Well... all right." I did so, hoping this wouldn't get me in trouble in any additional life I might be entitled to later. (It hasn't so far.)

I was issued a stylish grasshopper-green uniform and entered the army officially as Private F. Burly 0775321. Which is ironic in a way because that's the same number I was assigned in the Death House later on. But I've got to remember not to get ahead of my story. That's bad storytelling. It tips off the reader about what is coming. So just forget what I just said about the Death House, and my lucky escape in the garbage truck.

Along with the other new recruits, I was loaded onto a green troop bus and transported to nearby Ray Walston Army Training Base for boot camp.

The war spirit on the bus was high. Everyone was bragging about all the heroic things they were planning on doing in the war (no one was planning on being a coward or screwing up, I noticed), telling each other which Earth celebrities they were going to blow away (they all had Orson Welles on their list), and having light-hearted gun battles with soldiers on other troop busses. There was a definite lack of discipline on that bus. I frowned a little at that. No one dislikes going to war, but soldiers shouldn't be too happy. It's bad for morale.

When we reached the camp we were assigned to our barracks. To my dismay, my platoon seemed to have gotten the real oddball recruits – the stupid, the lazy, the untrainable, the party boys, the clumsy. I complained to the senior officers about being thrown in with a bunch of 8-balls. Obviously a mistake had been made on the army's part. Let's get this situation sorted out and try to be more on the ball next time, I told them. They said no mistake had been made. I was placed in the right platoon. Boy that made me stop and think. That took the starch out of me. Apparently I was an 8-ball too.

I certainly seemed like an 8-ball once we had started our basic training. All the other recruits could run for miles and hop over obstacles like grasshoppers. I couldn't even get over the first obstacle. I still haven't gotten over it. It worried me that I wasn't making a better showing. I knew I wasn't built like most Martians, but I was a Martian, gosh darnit, so I should be able to do these things.

My frustration was compounded by the lackadaisical way the other men in the platoon went about their training. They didn't seem to be taking army life seriously at all. They wore their own custom-made outfits, spurning the "uniform look" preferred by the army. Some were dressed better than the Generals. And they used their mental powers to get out of a lot of their training. They'd make the drill sergeant think they were out on the drill field doing pushups, when actually they were still back in the barracks, doing pushups in their bunks. This sort of unmilitary behavior drove the officers crazy, but there were too many goof-offs to deal with. So they basically did nothing.

The goofing off offended me even more than it did the officers. Partly because I was programmed to be very patriotic now, but mostly because I didn't have the kind of imagination required to goof off like the others were doing. I had the sort of standard issue imagination; the kind that allows you to tie your shoes or eat meat. It was my feeling that if I had to do it, they had to do it.

When I realized that the officers weren't going to do anything to stop the goofing off, I did something myself. I started cuffing the recruits around when they slacked off and told them to get going and make me and Mars proud of them or else. Frightened by my bulk, my bad grammar and my psychotic attitude, they obeyed. The ones who didn't, got it good. I kicked one guy in the ass so hard part of his face fell off. That scared everybody. Me too (the guy's face fell off!), but I didn't show it.

They started calling me the "Camp Bully", or "Bully Burly". I didn't mind. Hell, I was a bully. Might as well face facts.

Finally I was called in to the Captain's office. He told me that I had been observed bullying the men on several occasions.

"Yes sir. Fifty occasions."

He counted the reports and nodded. Yes, it was fifty.

"Will that be all, sir?"

"No!"

He told me that the reports indicated that this bullying had been successful.

"Yes sir. One guy's face fell off, but aside from that..."

"Army regulations strictly prohibit this kind of bullying, Private Burly."

I saluted. "Will that be all, sir?"

"No!" said the Captain. "Because Privates are not allowed to discipline the other soldiers, I'm promoting you to Acting Corporal. Then when you bully the men you will be acting according to the rulebook."

I was going to ask if that was all, but I decided not to. I had been burned twice before. So I kept my mouth shut.

"That's all, Corporal Burly."

"Thank you, sir."

I began training the 20 troopers assigned to me with great enthusiasm. Now we could get something done! I didn't really know how to train a platoon, but I figured I could pick it up as I went along. The important thing was to show leadership at all times. I paraded the men up and down the drill field, shouting commands never heard before or since: "Different directions...march!", "Come back... ho!", "Both directions... now!", "Up march!", "Down go!", Platoon... fly!"

The men hesitated to follow some of my stranger sounding orders at first, but I taught them to obey without question. Army men aren't used to being poisoned or burned at the stake by their own leaders. So that got their attention. They learned to fear me.

One rich snooty recruit didn't like the way I kicked him around. I said I didn't care whether he liked it or not. I liked it, and that was all that was important. He said he would have me shot if I kept it up. And you know what? He did!

After I got out of the hospital I was kind of afraid to go back to my platoon, but I found out that the rich kid had deserted by then. I didn't go look for him. They said it would be a black mark on my record if I didn't find him, but I said I liked black. So that ended that argument.

After a couple of weeks I had my men trained well enough so that they would obey my orders to the letter without thinking. This sometimes resulted in them marching off a cliff, or somehow leaving the planet's thin atmosphere. Then I had to ask the Captain for more recruits. He didn't like that, and neither one of us liked all the additional paperwork that had to be done, but I always ended up getting my new recruits. There were plenty of them available. The war was very popular at this point because no one had gotten hurt yet.

Even with all the mistakes I was making – all the unexplained deaths and clumsy cover-ups, and all the damage I was doing to the army base – my platoon was progressing while the others in camp were getting worse.

Respect for authority was on the decline in a lot of the platoons. The words "Ah shaddap" were frequently heard after an order was given. The troops thought the officers were "squares". They had to be taught that maybe being a "square" was "cool". They asked how that could be. I said that I said "MAYBE". Besides, I told them, maybe it's "hip" not to ask questions. Maybe it's "hip" to do what you're told. To be obedient. And docile. To not have a mind of your own. Maybe that's what's "hip" these days. Most of the troops hadn't thought of that. It was a new and false sounding idea to them. I think that helped me keep the men in line – talking so crazy like that.

Since my platoon was plainly the most professional in camp, the higher-ups promoted me again so I could bring my brand of "Burly Discipline" to more platoons.

As my confidence in my leadership abilities grew, I no longer bothered drilling the men myself. I left that to underlings who knew what they were doing and could tell their left feet from their neighbor's left feet, while I concentrated on the larger issues. I taught the men in my battalion to be just like the Old Man (me). I taught them to be tenacious, self-absorbed, single-minded, and tough. And, of course, I inadvertently taught them my weaknesses: to be petty and obnoxious, to panic in a crisis, to be late for work, everything I knew.

I taught my men to go straight towards their objective, over any obstacle, no matter how high or how easy to go around. ("The Burly Maneuver") That way we didn't need maps or strategy or sense of direction of any kind. Feet is all we needed. Good old Martian feet. It's an easy strategy to remember, and it also saves on map printing costs. When you've got an army to run, you've got to worry about everything.

With each batch of men I successfully trained, I got more men, and a new promotion.

On April 30th at 6 am, I watched proudly as my men marched across the tarmac, climbing over luggage carts and airport workers, and boarded their saucers for the invasion. An invasion which was to be commanded by General Xxpmpt, Air Marshal Rrogyx, and Lance General (recently promoted from Buck General) Burly – that's me.

It was an impressive invasion fleet that was being assembled on that field. Our saucers not only contained thousands of highly trained fighting men, their cargo bays were loaded with all kinds of scary sounding battle machines: Galaxy Smashers, Earth Shatterers, and Life Snuffers. And new wonder weapons like the

Soldier Thrower which could hurl a fully armed soldier two hundred yards towards the enemy, and the bigger version of the same machine: the deadly General Launcher.

As I watched the last Planet Pincher being rolled aboard, I was surprised to see Arthur Gremlin appear at my side. I hadn't seen him in a long time. And according to my brainwashing, had never seen him. I tried to reconcile these two facts, but my brain was just making cuckoo clock sounds. (Again!). Gremlin told me he had been assigned to be my staff assistant and would be there to help me and watch me wherever I went and whatever I did. I welcomed him aboard. It always helps to have someone watching you to make sure you do the right thing. That's the first thing they teach a young Martian like me. He hissed his way on board and sat down in the seat next to mine.

Now that I had been living on Mars for awhile, it was easy for me to see that Arthur Gremlin was different from other Martians. It was a subtle difference, but it was there. As we were waiting to take off, I asked him about it.

"I notice you're different from the rest of us Martians," I said. "Bone structure or something. And the shade of green is a little different."

"Yes. I'm from 'the country'."

I didn't see what difference that would make. Then I realized it was probably a euphemism.

"Oh, I get it. You're a member of an inferior race."

"Well I wouldn't put it quite that way."

"Too complicated a thought for your people to understand?"

"Not really."

"Maybe if you just tried harder you wouldn't be so inferior. That's what I do."

"Yes. Thank you. Could we launch the attack now please?"

I nodded and gave the signal to lift off.

CHAPTER TEN

Our mighty invasion fleet hurtled through space. It was the most magnificent array of battle machines Mars had ever assembled. No matter what you think an alien spaceship should look like, we had one of those.

Inside my flagship spirits were high. The troops were singing anti-Earth songs like "We'll Hang Joe Earth From A Sour Apple Tree", and stirring Martian anthems like "Here We Go, Martians, Here We Go!"

Some of my troops were passing the time by reading my memoirs, which told of my impoverished youth on Mars and my rapid rise to General, adding a number of exaggerations and falsehoods to make it sound better. (I didn't invent moveable type! I forget who did, but I'm pretty sure it wasn't me.) Also included in a special section of this book were the famous quotes attributed to me (but actually they were just quotes I vaguely remembered hearing back on Earth). Quotes like: "When Things Get Rough, The Rough Get Things", "Never Meet A

Man That You Don't Like", and "Loose Lips Lookout Below!" The troops would repeat these quotes to each other and then say to me: "Good quote, sir." And I would smile. I tried to encourage this kind of brown-nosing in my outfit. It was good for my morale. I made a mental note that if I ever needed my ass kissed for any reason – it might be a medically-related reason or some other reason – these were the boys to do it.

As we got deeper into space and the long confinement and the usual war nerves started to get to some of the men, rumors started going around that the enemy would be using real bullets, not just practice bullets like the men were used to. And that our Generals were pompous buffoons who were leading us to our doom. And that Mars didn't have any real quarrel with Earth, we were just pawns of those bastards on Neptune. And that there had been a shakeup in the Army's ranking system and Privates now outranked the King.

I listened to this for awhile, then started a rumor that everybody had better shut-up. They did, but they weren't happy about following orders from me now. The rumor was, I was a pompous buffoon.

As they lapsed into a sullen silence, I felt it was time to launch into the stirring speech I had prepared. The one that began: "I think it was Benedict Arnold who said..." I was hampered in my speech-making by the fact that I had come down with the Martian Flu the day before we took off, and it was getting worse by the hour. I kept coughing on my audience, which they dutifully applauded along with everything else that came out of my mouth, but I could tell it was lessening the overall effect of my speech. Things really went downhill though, when I got past the opening jokes, and the pointing out of the prominent enlisted men in the audience tonight, and got into the meat of the speech.

"Many of you won't be coming back," I began.

There was great alarm at this. What was this all about? Nobody mentioned not coming back before. I guess I shouldn't have said that. They thought we were all coming back. Now they weren't sure they wanted to go. Not if they weren't coming back. I had to get back the ground I had lost. I did this by lying.

"You didn't let me finish. What I was trying to tell you was, many of you won't be coming back empty-handed!"

"Yay!"

"You'll be coming back with pockets full of cash!"

"Hurrah!"

"No, wait men. Not yet. Wait for the order. We're still up in space someplace."

My troops stopped trying to yank open the doors and sat back down, rubbing their hands at the thought of all the money they were going to make on this deal. I tossed the rest of my speech away. The men were fired up enough.

From then on I kept my speeches short, false, and money oriented.

As we got within a half million miles of Earth, we tested out the ship's guns and got in some target practice by destroying several probes from other galaxies that were on their way to Earth with good news for everyone. We probably shouldn't have done that, now that I think about it. But you've got to have targets if you want to have target practice.

With its guns primed and ready, the mighty Martian fleet raised its battle flag, crossed its fingers, and dove into the Earth's atmosphere.

Here is where I should say I had a plan to save the Earth, so I guess here is where I'm going to have to be honest. I didn't have a plan to save the Earth. I was attacking the Earth, me and my Martian buddies.

At a radar tracking station in Honolulu, the aged radar man who had ignored the approaching Japanese fleet at Pearl Harbor, noticed the approaching Martian fleet, and ignored it. It wasn't that he didn't recognize the danger, it's just that he had a reputation to uphold.

Moments later, everyone saw us. Regular broadcasting was suspended and live television broadcasts zeroed in on the Martian saucers streaking towards Earth, guns blazing.

Anxious news-anchors appeared on camera, trying to make the invasion sound more interesting than it was. Some said our death rays might be infected with smallpox. Others worried that we might be bringing the dinosaurs back. They all had their own frightening, ratings-raising theories.

"So this is the end," said one. "Many of us here in the newsroom felt the world would end this way. And now it's happening. Just in time for me to win my bet."

Earth leaders were mystified by this sudden attack. Urgent messages went out on all frequencies to try to establish contact with the mysterious invaders.

"Attention invading fleet," asked a calm measured voice. "Aren't you going to give the Earth some kind of warning? Because we're used to getting warnings first." Then, after there was no response, a more hysterical sounding radio operator, with a higher pitched voice, was brought in to repeat the question.

When there was no response from the menacing craft, except to turn up their theremins, the people of Earth began to panic. Everyone began to run, ignoring the fact that they were running around on the target.

A cable news tracking poll taken at the height of the hysteria showed that 67% of Americans said they were running as fast as they could, while 32% felt they could run faster.

Earth's leaders weren't running. They were diving into underground bunkers which had been specially prepared for moments just like this. Everywhere people went they saw government officials hiding under or behind things. I guess that's what makes them leaders, hiding like that.

Earth defenses sprang into action. Supersonic jets shot up into the sky from nearly every nation on Earth. Missiles were launched from land, sea and air. The Martian fleet suddenly found itself flying through a sky filled with bad-tempered jets, deadly missiles and massive explosions.

The first skirmish was a revelation to the leaders on both sides. The Martian saucers were not only armed to the teeth, with energy beams that never seemed to run down, their pilots could employ their mental powers to make the devastation seem even worse than it was. Many enemy pilots bailed out of planes that hadn't been hit at all.

On the other hand, the Earth forces were setting off explosions that made the Martians' death rays seem like parlor tricks by comparison.

On board my flagship, the Chiefs of Staff started giving me worried looks – worried looks I've grown to recognize as Worried Look #4 and Worried Looks #s 7-25. I was the source of a lot of their information about Earth weaponry, and we were all starting to worry I might have been seriously full of shit.

After the battle had been raging for nearly an hour, it became obvious to everyone that the Martians were overmatched. Their stylish but underpowered weapons and mind control methods and magic tricks, which were dazzling at first, and still good at short range or on the stage, were nothing compared to the titanic explosions Earth science had developed.

Our saucers broke out of what was increasingly looking like a losing battle in the air and came in low to start strafing things on the ground. People were running from us in terror, with me pointing out the best targets. "There's an Earthman there!" I would yell. "His name is Jerry! Get him!"

I had briefed the other saucer pilots about targets of importance they would find on Earth besides the usual military bases, missile silos and so on. So there was a lot of fighting around the Alamo and Iwo Jima.

Some of the ships in my wing spent too much time chasing after and strafing one gangster who kept dodging them and firing back as he ran, downing three saucers before he was nailed by a hail of death rays. As he died he started saying something that sounded like "Crime does not pay" or "You were right all along, Father O'Malley", some important speech like that, but our saucers were long gone by then. So I don't know for sure which one of those two things he said.

I wasted my share of valuable time too. I tried to use my death ray to replace George Washington's face on Mount Rushmore with my own face, but you know, that's harder than it sounds. It's not enough to be a brutal trigger-happy maniac with no sense of history, you've got to be an artist as well. There haven't been many guys like that. Hitler and Rembrandt are the only ones I can think of. I finally got the face to look something like me, but by then the mountain was only two feet high. The tourists didn't like that. They kept tripping over it.

Our saucers were circling the Earth at tree-top level, blasting everything that moved and a lot of things that didn't. Even if we weren't exactly winning, we were sure scaring the hell out of everybody, and doing a lot of damage.

Teams of government experts, who must not have had much to do up until now, were called in to figure out how to deal with us. This was their moment. Now they would start earning all that pay they had been getting all these years.

They captured one of our men, pulling him out of a downed saucer, and examined him to find our weaknesses biologically. Fortunately for us, the man they captured was a professional boxer known as "Rufus, The Martian Strongboy". After a lengthy examination, in the course of which they received several bloody noses and had all of their eyes blackened, they determined that the Earth should fight somebody else. Martians were dynamite.

After having taken considerably more losses in the air than we expected, we finally managed to get our troops onto the ground for the land battle. After all, you can't surrender to a flying saucer. You have to surrender to the space monster that slithers out of it.

I put down my saucer a few miles outside of Central City. We slithered out and immediately ran into some teenagers who were necking in a convertible. The girls were horrified by our appearance and screamed so much we had to drag them into our saucer to get them to shut-up.

My men liked the way they could make teenage Earth girls scream.

"Let's make more girls scream," said one of them.

"Aye aye, Private," said another.

"Belay that order," I said sternly. "We've got work to do."

We formed into columns and struck out for the city. We met little resistance at first; a few small Earth scouting parties, a suspicious farmer who we finally managed to kill, and a few more teenage girls. So before long we could claim a string of unimportant, but important, victories.

The main reason for these victories was my battle strategy, or lack of same, which I've already described to you (The Burly Maneuver). I kept my men going straight for our objective, ignoring the roads and bridges, climbing trees we easily could have walked around, and so on. This is unorthodox, because it is a bad idea, and it confuses the enemy, who were expecting to be fighting something that made sense. Think again, Earthman.

Since the Earthmen knew they were fighting aliens from another planet, they tried various experimental methods to defeat us. They tried different sound frequencies on me but none of them worked. I like sound frequencies. Nonetheless, I discouraged that sort of thing as much as I could. You never know – the next crackpot idea might work. "Form a protective cordon around me men," I told my boys. "We can't afford to lose me. I'm getting paid the most."

As we got closer to the city, we ran up against fewer suspicious farmers and more trained troops. During these battles I kept coughing on the enemy by mistake as I was fighting with them. That Martian Flu just wouldn't go away.

"Sorry," I said as I coughed repeatedly in an attacker's face. "Sorry. Sorry."

"Cough the other way when you're fighting can't you?"

"I'll try."

But in the heat of the battle, I often forgot to cough the other way.

The more I fought and coughed, the more the enemy troops started to cough.

The battles had all gone our way at first, but in the long run being unorthodox is no match for knowing what you're doing, so soon my various battle groups began losing. The enemy would hide behind a tree, for example, then wait for my men to start climbing it. Then they would set fire to that tree.

My subordinates were afraid to tell me when things started to go wrong. They started bringing in overly optimistic battle reports.

"How'd that battle go, Lieutenant?"

"Great!"

"Is there something wrong with your leg?"

"No, it's great."

"Because it looks like it's bleeding."

"...it's great."

Well, warfare shouldn't be all work. It's bad for morale. Since we were winning so handily, according to the glowing reports I had been getting, I decided to show my men I was a regular guy just like them, not the battle hardened thinking machine I appeared to be.

"Since everything's going so great, Lieutenant, order the men to put down all their weapons in a big pile and have a party."

"Uh..." He hesitated.

I became impatient. "Now, Lieutenant."

"Yes sir."

Before the party could really get going, while the first record was still playing in fact, we were attacked again. This time in force. We quickly found ourselves pinned down and being fired upon from all sides.

I began firing off commands: "Third Battle Group – stop dancing!... Burly's Rangers – turn off that music!... All units – find your weapons!"

My men began sorting through the pile of weapons for theirs. Meanwhile, more Earth columns began arriving and joining in on what was turning out to be a turkey shoot.

The commander of the Earth forces didn't enjoy shooting down people who were wearing party hats. It didn't seem right to him somehow. He ordered his troops to stop firing, then demanded our surrender.

Since our situation was obviously hopeless at this point, my men began unhappily putting down their glasses of punch and surrendering. I couldn't believe it. My boys had let me down. Then I found myself surrendering too. I couldn't believe that either.

But we still had an ace up our sleeve. An ace we didn't even know about.

As we were being marched to Area 51 to be secretly imprisoned, our captors suddenly started feeling sick. It was the Martian Flu and it was spreading quickly through the ranks. Fortunately, my men weren't affected. All Martians are vaccinated against the Martian Flu at birth. Occasionally, one child is passed over, as must have happened in my case, but most Martians never get the unpleasant disease.

As the stricken Earthmen started doubling over, they sent off coughing messengers to alert other Earth battalions of this new danger.

Soon we weren't being marched anywhere anymore. Our captors were lying on their backs, throwing up on their equipment, and hollering for thermometers.

Delighted, my men confiscated all of the enemy's weapons and we began marching them in to the city.

When we got there, we found that everyone in Central City had also come down with what was beginning to be known as the Burly Flu. They were quick to surrender when we promised them hot water bottles and something warm to put over their shoulders.

The Burly Flu was spreading rapidly around the world. Nothing could be done to stop it or even slow it down. Medical science knew nothing about it. It didn't seem to be a virus or any kind of bacteria they had ever seen. They didn't even know where to start. Great professors from the worlds of physics, biology and astronomy were called in to try to find the key to this baffling alien disease, but they couldn't figure it out either. And pretty soon people stopped calling them "Professor" and started calling them "Dimwit" or "Jerkoff".

Meanwhile, the Martian Army marched on, taking city after city, usually without firing a shot. All they usually had to do was give the opposing army some Kleenex and a nice place to lie down and the battle was over.

When it looked like America was about to surrender, I was there to spot the phony and say: "That's not the real President!" It turned out it was the real President. I had forgotten about the last couple of elections. The guy I was thinking of wasn't even alive anymore. I guess I should read the papers more.

So the Martians had won. And it was the smallest thing the Martian God Zog had created – germs – that was the undoing of the Earthmen.

The great Martian victory celebration began. There were handshakes and slaps on the back all around, congratulatory phone calls from dignitaries back home, and parades of marching troops and flower-covered flying saucers down the Main Street of every important city. I rode in the vanguard of as many parades as I could.

The only one not joining in the merriment was Arthur Gremlin. I slapped him on the back to get him into the party spirit, but he just hissed, rubbed his back, and said he had phone calls to make. I didn't mind, really. Even though we were both on the same team, and great buddies officially, the guy gave me the creeps.

At the end of that exciting first week of the Martian Occupation, a special ceremony was held to honor me. I was congratulated for my brilliant military victory and was made a Triple Double General, which on Mars is the equivalent of an Octuple Movie Star. I was now 4th in line to be King of Mars.

"Well, that worked out pretty well," I said to the press. "I guess all's well that ends well. Assuming this is the end, of course."

CHAPTER ELEVEN

The Martians quickly turned the Earth into one big manufacturing and slave colony. Soon it was the number one exporter of feeler covers, cheap trinkets, grasshopper food, and green paint in the Solar System.

All Earthmen had to work in Martian sweatshops, in slave-like conditions. There was no longer any free will. No one had even a shred of human dignity. All Earthmen had to jump when the Martians said jump. The Martians quite enjoyed this and used the word "jump" in their sentences a lot when there were Earthmen within hearing.

"I hear you JUMPED into the semi-conductor market, Jerry."

"Yes, I JUMPED at the chance to JUMP into that."

"Let's sing the "JUMP-JUMP Song".

"Okay."

"JUMP-JUMP-JUMP-JUMP..."

All through this, long-suffering Earthmen

would be tragically springing into the air in all directions.

Of course there was some resistance to this slavery and degradation. Bricks were thrown through windows. Policemen were pushed over. There was even the occasional deadly explosion. None of it was very big, but the irritation to the Martians was cumulative. That is to say, it accumulated.

The Martians had to delegate a lot of their resources to chase after the troublemakers. They caught some of them, but most of them just disappeared somewhere. It was suggested that these underground fighters might be living underground someplace, but this suggestion was viewed as too simplistic.

"The world is more complicated than that, Jenkins," said one high official, gruffly.

"I realize that now, sir."

"Stop living in a dream world."

"Consider it done, sir."

Since there were no actual wars to fight anymore, most of the army was demobilized and I was given a new job. A job that fit in perfectly with my powerful physique and short temperment. I was put in charge of kicking slaves in the ass to get them going. And believe me there were plenty of Earth slaves who needed to get going.

This was a great job for a guy like me, a dream job, except there was no room for advancement. You couldn't move up to kicking more important people's asses. Or something more important than asses, like, I dunno, museums or something. I was kind of stuck where I was professionally. Still, I was good at it, so I enjoyed it.

I kicked the downtrodden. I beat up the poor. I slapped the helpless. And people yearning to breath free I walloped good.

"You'll never beat the little people," a few defiant slaves assured me.

"I'll beat you then," I replied, and started doing so.

Sometimes as I walloped I got to wondering if I was still the good guy here, but then I decided I was. I was just a good guy with a dark side. An edgy kind of good guy. A good guy with an attitude. Like a Bargain Basement Humphrey Bogart.

I did try, whenever possible, to be a benevolent and kind-hearted ass-kicker.

"Do not think of yourselves as prisoners," I told my charges kindly. "You are free to move about just as freely as you always... get back here! I'm not finished. You are free to move about... god dammit get back here! I'm going to kick your asses so hard..."

Like I said, it was a good job and I was good at it, so I guess my story would have finally come to its happy ending right about here if I hadn't suddenly found myself kicking some old friends one morning: Dottie and Chuck Steak. Of course I didn't recognize them right away. To a Martian like me they were just more slaves. All Earthmen look alike to us. Did you ever notice that? They greeted me joyously and, between kicks, asked me why wasn't I detecting things? Why was I kicking them instead? I didn't know what they were talking about, and told them so in a kind of kicking code I had developed.

Dottie thought I must have amnesia again. Chuck was sure of it. So, when I had my back turned to slap somebody whose face I suddenly didn't like, they bashed me repeatedly over the head with their shovels. It was then that I discovered that hard blows to the head might not work for amnesia, but they work great for brainwashing. I could suddenly remember everything. I looked down and saw I was wearing Martian clothes and kicking Earthmen. So far, so good.

I noticed a slave who was lagging behind the others. His aged hands were nearly useless for digging. I gave him a couple of kicks to remedy that. "Dig faster, asshole."

"Ah-SHOLEY," he said, automatically correcting the pronunciation.

I looked at him more closely. It was my old landlord!

"Help me, Burly. It's your old pal, Jack Asshole."

"Are you going to lower my rent?"

"Never!"

"Then keep digging."

I was glad to see that I had managed, after all that had happened to me, to land on my feet. But was the rest of my life this good? Over the next few days I discovered that it wasn't.

My Martian-provided apartment, now that I could see it through un-brainwashed eyes, if you follow me, was crap. I had no possessions beyond some style-less State-provided clothing and a small lamp that told me when to go to bed, made me do calisthenics every morning, and I'm pretty sure ate some of my food.

The Martians kept everybody working all the time. Even big-shots like me. They had a pill that kept you alert and working hard day and night. And they had another pill that made you take that first pill.

There were propaganda trucks roaming the streets 24 hours a day, blaring out uplifting slogans like: "Work is Not Work. At Least Not Anymore.", "Slavery Is Freedom, Even Though They Appear To Be Spelled Differently", and "Get Back To Work".

There was a painting of the Martian Military Governor on the wall of my apartment which stared at me all the time and occasionally asked me where I was going, or what I had there in my hand. When I found its presence had gotten a little tiring, I asked for it to be removed. The next day forty more identical paintings were installed in my apartment. So now they could not only watch me everywhere in the apartment, they could watch me from many exciting different angles. And they could watch each other too. And have long loud conversations with each other that kept me awake at night.

Every time I tried to take one of these paintings down it screamed and started yelling for guards to come help the painting – the painting was in trouble. So I left them up.

Curfew was from dusk to dawn. And then again from dawn to dusk. That didn't leave much time for screwing around. I tried pointing that out to the sentries but they just pointed to their watches and said it was past curfew. They said if I didn't know what time it was they would gladly burn the current time into my forehead. I said no, that was all right. I guess I'd buy a watch.

I hadn't had a watch since my friends had broken mine, banging me over the head with it to cure my amnesia.

I went to the old Earth Quarter and found an antique shop that still sold watches. The Martians had phased out timepieces for personal use on the theory that slaves didn't need to know what time it was. For them it was always "time to work".

The shop didn't have anything fancy, but I finally found and purchased a serviceable watch. I also bought, on a whim, a diary.

At first most of what I wrote in this diary was pretty harmless – comments about the weather, what I had eaten that day, and which episode of "My Favorite Martian" I had watched on TV that night.

But soon I was using the pages to voice my concerns about the Martian Administration: "Martians are a little too ruthless and efficient for my taste," I wrote. "And they look a little too much like grasshoppers." I underlined "grasshoppers" and drew a finger pointing at it to draw attention to it. Then I put the word "nasty" in front of "grasshoppers". In retrospect I probably should have gone a little easier on all that insect stuff. I got the impression later that that offended them more than anything else I had written.

I bought some more diaries and wrote down my most important thoughts in each one. I still wasn't sure which one I preferred, so I kept buying them. When I finally decided which one was best, I didn't want to have to rewrite everything. I'm not stupid.

Of course I couldn't leave incriminating writing like that laying around in my apartment in plain view. So I hid them. Soon I had diaries squirreled away everywhere. I even hid a few of them behind the paintings. The faces in the paintings turned, trying to see what was behind them, but they couldn't quite do it. All of the hiding places I had chosen were good, but there were so many of them the floor was starting to buckle.

To solve this problem, I tied them all together and hung them out of my window. But I stopped doing that when I went outside and noticed they were dangling in front of my boss's window.

One night I came home and all of my diaries were gone! I looked accusingly at the nearest painting. The figure in the painting smirked.

I found the diaries the next morning. They were piled on the Military Governor's desk. And I was in front of it, looking worried.

"Do these diaries belong to you, Mr. Burly? They have your name on them."

"I cannot recall, your honor. Probably not. They're on your desk. My guess is, they're probably yours."

He picked up one of the diaries and read from it. "When you wrote 'The Martians are a pain in the neck, and the Governor is a big fat slob', what exactly did you mean by that Mr. Burly?"

This was a trick question, of course. My story, as both of us well knew, was that these weren't my diaries. He was being clever. I had to be just as clever. "I didn't mean those things I wrote," I said.

He stared at me for awhile, then dismissed me. So I figured I had bluffed my way successfully through that one. Score one for me. That's twelve now. But it was too close. The next time I might not be so clever.

A week passed without incident. The Governor said no more about my diaries, but I could sense that I wasn't as trusted a member of the administration as I had been before. My security clearances were all cancelled. And there were so many paintings in my room now the government had to add more walls. Time to go, Burly, I thought.

I surreptitiously started sending messages to the Earth Underground asking what kind of a deal I could get for switching sides. There didn't have to be a lot of money involved, I stressed. I wasn't trying to get rich on the deal.

Though, of course, any money they might have to offer would certainly help me make my decision.

My messages never got any farther than the Military Governor's desk. That's the Post Office for you. Each morning the Governor would read them and frown while he was having his morning coffee. As each day passed, more bags of them arrived, being dumped on his desk like letters to Santa Claus. As the Governor leafed through them, Arthur Gremlin would sit in the corner watching and hissing.

I kept checking my mail, but I never got an answer. I should have been getting thousands of replies. Something was wrong. I decided to try to contact the Underground in person. I took off my uniform and feelers and dressed up in some Earth-style clothes I found on a slave, then headed for the Earth Quarter. Thanks to my unusual build and the fact that I was actually born on Earth, I felt I could pass myself off as an Earthman easy enough.

As I walked through the Earth Quarter, eyes turned to watch me. Hundreds of eyes. There were eyes lined up for blocks. Finally I got tired of it and poked a couple of those eyes. That stopped that for awhile.

I told people I needed to contact the Earth Underground. They asked me why. Thinking fast, I said it owed me money. I hadn't been paid for some tunnels. They said there was no such thing as the Earth Underground. I said then who has been blowing up all us Martians' stuff? They didn't have an answer to that. That shut them up. But I still didn't know where the Earth Underground was.

Since no one would help me, I decided the only thing to do was to stand next to something important until it blew up and then try to remember who did it. The only problem with this idea is that it's hard to remember things when you've just been blown halfway across the street. I was forgetting the information as fast as I was getting it.

After I'd been blown up a half a dozen times and was standing determinedly in front of an arsenal, one of the Earthmen took pity on me. He sidled up to me and handed me a business card, then hurried off. I looked at the card. It was for the Earthman Club Café. On the back of the card was written in pencil "Go to the Earthman Club Café". The same message was written carefully along the edges. Somebody wanted me to go to the Earthman Club Café.

I knew where the café was. It was right between the "Don't Go Here Café" and the "Not This One Either Café" What I didn't know until I got there was that it was a major meeting place for leaders of the Underground.

I went in and sat down at a small table in the back and waited, only occasionally yelling "Hey! Where's the Earth Underground?" and "I haven't got all day like the cops do."

Finally an enormous shadowy figure approached my table and, without introducing himself, sat down and looked me over. "So it's the Underground you're looking for, is it?"

"Yes. Is that you?"

"You flatter me. Let's say that I'm its most visible outer manifestation."

"Okay, we'll say that. But from now on let's try to use smaller words."

Before we could get any deeper into our conversation, the band struck up a theme. The fat man stood up.

"My music. You'll excuse me for a few moments, I'm sure. It wouldn't do to have our Martian friends think I was anything more than just a humble entertainer."

He went up on stage and began singing gibberish while the other performers whacked him over the head with oversized mallets.

"Gibberty gibberty gib-gib-gib!
That's what I always say!
Weeza weeza weeza wheeeeee!
What do you think of me now?"

His number ended with him staggering around the stage, blinded by the constant attacks, finally letting loose with a big roundhouse punch that knocked his own teeth out.

He came back to the table, bowing slightly to the audience to acknowledge the applause. Then, after removing his fright wig and skunk tail and spinning his eyes back to where they were before, he sat down.

"Now we can talk," he said.

"Maybe I should talk to somebody else."

That's when the Martian police came up to

my table. "You could talk to us, General Burly."

Heads turned at the mention of my name. The fat man looked startled.

One of the policemen reached out to grab me. I had to think fast.

"Get back!" I warned him. "Just one word from me and that dog will tear you to pieces."

"What dog?"

I took off running. He had called my bluff about the dog. I hadn't seen a dog in weeks.

As I crashed through the club, knocking over tables and waiters and people who were trying to help me, I appealed to the people of Earth to rise up and overthrow their alien overlords, starting with the alien overlords who were trying to grab me by the scruff of the neck.

"Kill them!" I pleaded wildly. "Revolution! Won't somebody stop these dirty filthy smelly Martians?"

As the dirty filthy smelly Martians handcuffed me and started leading me away, I told them I wasn't a traitor. It was all a joke. They said it wasn't a very good joke, and I said humor was very subjective, stupid. If they were smart they would know that. What's funny to one person is treason to another. And vice versa. That got us discussing comedy theory and forgetting my treason for awhile.

Finally the leader got tired of it. "Never mind about Abbott and Costello. Let's go."

My trial didn't last very long. Martian law says you can't defend someone in court unless you actually believe he's innocent. They want defendants to get a fair trial, but they don't want to have to listen to a bunch of bullshit. That meant no lawyer could defend me. Everybody knew I was guilty. So I had to defend myself.

I'm glad I've never had to try to make my living as a lawyer. It's harder than driving a bus, I think. The prosecution had me in a hole right from the start.

"Are these letters to the Earth Underground which refer to the Martian people as 'insect-faced degenerates' signed by you?" the prosecutor demanded.

"Yes!"

This admission caused a sensation in the court. After I had finished tipping my hat to the excited crowd, I realized I shouldn't have admitted that.

"No further questions," said the prosecutor.

"Wait a minute, I meant yes, BUT..."

"You may step down," said the judge.

"My sentence isn't over, your majesty."

I tried to explain to the court that I hadn't finished my sentence yet. At least let me finish my stinking sentence. But they didn't want to hear anymore. The admission of guilt was enough. I could step down now.

I stepped down, but I didn't like it. What about the rest of my sentence?

As I was walking back to my seat, the judge, with a happy inspiration, said I would be able to finish my "sentence" soon enough. A "sentence" of "prison time". Then he wrecked it by laughing too loud and too long at his own joke.

The case for the defense was hamstrung from the start by the fact that I was guilty of all the things I was charged with, and more. Still, I gave it the old college try.

I tried to tell the court about my troubled childhood, and how little my parents encouraged me and how many miles I had to walk just to sneak a smoke, or slug a smaller boy, but they grew impatient. They weren't interested in my past, and didn't like me at any age. I said if they would let me continue, I was just about to get to my troubled teenage years, some of which were R rated. But the judge overruled this whole line of reminiscences. He wanted to talk about the trial.

Now I'd seen enough TV shows about trials to know that you've got to surprise 'em. The lawyer who wins is the lawyer with the biggest surprises. So I showed up wearing different clothes everyday. And one day I stood in a completely different spot. (There's that imagination problem I was telling you about). These were pretty surprising surprises, I thought. But the prosecution lawyer surprised everybody even more by how much evidence he had against me.

When it came time for the summing up, I laid out all of my evidence, reminded the court that I was still offering that bribe I had mentioned, then said to the judge: "You be the judge. You decide."

"Guilty," he said instantly. "Prisoner is sentenced to death."

I thought about this. "I'll be the judge. I'll decide."

"Take him away."

"Objection, your honor," I said. I objected to being taken away.

"Denied."

"Well, shit..."

I was taken to a maximum security prison to await my execution. They slammed my cell door shut, then slammed it a couple of more times until they felt they had made their point. Then they left me alone to face my doom.

"Objection," I said.

CHAPTER TWELVE

My first few days of confinement in a maximum security prison were probably the low point of my life. I had to memorize my new name, which was 0775321, learn the daily prison routine, get the hang of my new job in the prison laundry, meet my new cellmates, all of whom had colorful hard-to-remember names like Strangler and Knifey, all kinds of learning and memorizing. It made my head hurt. I wished I was dead, then remembered I soon would be. That should have cheered me up, but it didn't.

I managed to keep my spirits up by singing loudly in my cell all night long. And imitating a trombone. I learned Latin, which I've always been meaning to do, but never had the time; then forgot it, which I always figured would happen.

But no matter how high my spirits got, they always came crashing down again when I noticed the calendar. The date of my execution had already been set, and the more I sang in my cell, the more they moved it up. I decided

I'd better stop trying to make the best of things and start trying to get the hell out of here. But I knew it wouldn't be easy. If it was easy, I would be alone in here. Everybody would have escaped already.

I asked around. The other prisoners didn't know of any way to escape off hand, but said if I found one they would appreciate being told about it. Otherwise they'd kill me. The warden was no help. He wouldn't even discuss the subject. So I asked a guard.

"Settle a bet for me," I said casually, pretending this was just a gambling question. "If someone wanted to knock your stupid head in and escape – this is a hypothetical question, you understand..."

"Yes, go on."

"How would he do it? When do you usually look the other way? And what's the quickest easiest way out of here once you've been disposed of?"

The guard wasn't very helpful on this score. He didn't think knocking him on the head would work. Even if a prisoner did get past him, there were other guards. And locked doors. And searchlights and vicious dogs. The prison was escape-proof. Knocking him on the head would just be a waste of time, in his opinion. He advised against it.

I realized I needed a better mind than mine working on this problem, so, as many people have before, I turned to the great minds of Hollywood. I went to the prison library and checked out an old 16mm copy of "The Great Escape". I had the prison projectionist run it over and over, while I took notes, occasionally asking him to run it back so I could watch various tunneling scenes again, and get ideas on shooting guards. I watched it so many times my captors started speaking a little German. Just a few words they had picked up like "schnell" and "raus".

Once I had a pretty good idea of how to proceed, all I needed were the proper tools.

One of the great things about being in prison is you can get practically anything from the guards in trade for cigarettes. Of course the guards aren't supposed to be providing this service, but everyone knows it's going on. It's an accepted feature of prison life everywhere. If a prison didn't have it, it probably couldn't compete.

When I told one of the guards I needed a shovel, he looked in all four directions to make sure no one was within earshot. Then, just to be sure, he looked in a fifth direction I hadn't noticed before.

"That's rather a tall order 0775321. What do you need a shovel for?"

I had to think fast. "I collect them," I said.

"May I see your collection?"

"No."

"Well, what particular kind of shovel do you need for your collection?"

"Doesn't matter."

"Hmmm."

"Better get me some dynamite too."

He looked at me questioningly.

"For my collection," I explained. "I might need to blow up my collection."

It ended up costing me 475 packs of cigarettes, but I finally got my shovel. The guard was nervous about being found out, but he felt it was worth the risk. He now had enough packs of cigarettes to retire.

The first tunnel I dug went under the prison showers, breaking all the pipes. So there was no more hot water in the showers. Just hot water everywhere else. Everybody was pretty mad about that. The next tunnel went straight into the warden's bedroom and up his right leg somehow. I was very embarrassed when I climbed out of that tunnel carrying my suitcase. I had a lot of explaining to do.

As my execution date grew closer, I dug more frantically. I even paid other prisoners to dig, and was negotiating with a local construction company. We had tunnels going everywhere. Eventually, as each tunnel was discovered, it had to be sealed up, with a guard posted in front of it, and another guard posted inside the tunnel in case you got past the first guard.

There were piles of dirt, busted up concrete, and broken pipes everywhere throughout the prison.

One of the guards tried to reason with me. "We realize you don't want to be imprisoned here," he assured me, "but we have problems too." He indicated all the debris he had just climbed over to get to me. "All this debris. And these pipes. All this construction equipment. It just makes everyone's life more difficult."

I said I was truly sorry, copper, and gave him my word I'd stop digging tunnels. But I didn't stop digging. I dug faster. I guess my word isn't worth much.

The other prisoners were as inconvenienced by all the construction work as the guards were, and made remarks to me I won't repeat here. Even the prison chaplain said I was a jerk. He said this wasn't just a personal opinion. He said he could prove it. He said he had found something in the Bible about it. That was disconcerting, but it didn't slow me down.

The more I tried to escape, the more everyone except me looked forward to the day of my execution. That's why it surprised everybody when I executed myself.

The one place in the prison that wasn't guarded at all was the execution chamber. It was felt that guards weren't necessary. Prisoners did not want to go there.

So one morning I just strolled in, stripped to my underwear, put my clothes in the electric chair and turned on the juice. When the clothes started to give off a nice charred smell, I turned off the current, got dressed, sat down in the chair, took a deep breath, and played dead.

I didn't have to wait long to be discovered. Electric chairs eat up a lot of current. When you fire them up, even for a few moments, every light in the prison dims under the load. Soon guards and prison officials were running into the death chamber from every direction. When they saw me in the chair, my clothes scorched, my body reeking, they knew I was dead.

They were wrong, but not by much. Back when I was living on Mars, I had worked hard to learn to cloud men's minds like all the other Martians could do. But every time I tried to do it, my mind would stop. Then my entire body would shut down and start to give off an intriguing smell. It happened so often, eventually my body got used to being shut down for awhile. So when the prison doctor checked me out, I appeared to be quite dead.

Of course there was a big uproar about the whole thing. Prisoners are supposed to be executed at the proper time in the proper way by the proper people. This free-lance stuff was out.

My last request, which they found on my body, was that I be put in a taxi cab, with the driver to be told to "just keep driving." They didn't honor that request. They didn't feel they owed me anything. Even in death I had pissed them off. So instead of the elaborate burial ceremony they had planned, they just tossed me in the prison dumpster. Kind of an insult, I remember thinking at the time.

The next day I was taken out with the rest of the trash in the back of a prison garbage truck. A guard on the main tower was alarmed when he saw me riding out face down in some old coleslaw.

"Hey! Isn't that a prisoner in the back of that truck?"

The other guard looked at me through his binoculars. "Oh, that's okay. That's Burly. He's garbage all right."

That stung, but I didn't say anything. I kept my mouth shut. You've got to know when to do that.

CHAPTER THIRTEEN

In my first few days as a fugitive from justice, I made a lot of beginner's mistakes, including: telling people I was a fugitive from justice, bragging about my clever escape to everyone I met, and running like hell from every policeman or fireman I saw. If you want to be a successful fugitive, I found, you don't run from the police. That just excites their curiosity. You hide from the police.

But hiding from the police isn't easy. It's not something you can just do. You need practice to get good at it. My first week on the run, practically everywhere the police looked, there I was. I hadn't yet mastered the manly art of hiding.

Poe said the best place to hide something was out in plain view where everyone could see it. I tried his theory a couple of times, hiding on top of a flagpole, in the middle of busy intersections, on the hoods of police cars, and on top of a statue of Edgar Allan Poe. But even though I was in plain view, as Poe stipulated, everybody saw me. No wonder Poe never made it as a criminal. His ideas were crap.

One mistake I made – and you can learn a valuable lesson from this, in case you're ever a fugitive – is that no matter how I disguised myself I always had the same face. That, I found out later, was one of the things that made me easy to spot. It was my face they were looking for. I wasted too much time trying to disguise my arms and legs. Never mind your arms and legs, I tell young fugitives. You can leave those the same. But you've got to change that face.

Another mistake I made was that whenever I adopted a new identity I always used the same name: Knarf Ylrub.

"How do you pronounce that?" people would ask.

"I dunno. It's 'Frank Burly' spelled backwards if that's any help to you. Try saying it standing on your head."

And I wasted a lot of time looking for the "Real Traitor". Finally I decided I was just kidding myself. It was me. I was the real traitor. I was going to have to come to grips with that, and move on.

The Fugitive Life is an unsettled life. I had to keep moving all the time, running from job to job and trap to trap. I seldom got far enough ahead of my pursuers to be able to sit down in a nice restaurant for dinner, for example. I had to run down the street eating a hot dog. Later, as the running got me into better shape, I would run down the street eating a salad. And don't even try to take a bath when you're on the run. The water goes all over the place.

I toiled at many jobs: fry cook, hired hand, janitor, dog breeder, political pundit, autograph authenticator.

Some I had to leave because I was no good at them. Some because I was in danger of being found out.

I'd be working in a diner, for example, and my description would start coming in over the radio. Everyone in the place would be listening and slowly realizing that each part of the description fit their brutal unfriendly fry cook. When this happened, I would slowly edge over to the radio, casually switch it off, unplug it, and carry it out back, where I would spend the rest of the morning burying it. These actions caused a lot of suspicion, but not as much suspicion as that radio was causing.

Other times my co-workers' suspicions would be aroused by items they found in my pockets when they were stealing from me, wanted posters with my face on them, my prison suit, that sort of thing, or by things I shouted in my sleep when I was sleeping on the job, like "you'll never catch me, coppers". Each time I would have to start running again before the police arrived.

And sometimes my near discovery was all my fault. Like when I tried to pass myself off as a member of the United States Supreme Court. They knew something was wrong when the morning head count revealed there were ten of us.

As my pursuers became more familiar with my modus operandi (I told you I learned Latin), I had to leave these jobs sooner. I was a mailman for only eight minutes – only long enough to flip out once – before the police kicked down the door of the Post Office. And my career as a heart surgeon only lasted long enough to remove one heart. And I had to throw that at the cops.

As I ran out of the hospital, along with a couple of other fugitives who were dressed as administrative personnel, I could sense the end of my chase was coming. Each day it seemed like more people were out looking for me. And I was running out of places to hide.

As I was trying to figure out my next move, and wondering if maybe I should hide in that electric chair again, they wouldn't expect to find me there, I suddenly noticed I was heading right towards a Martian patrol. I stopped and turned, but there was another patrol coming from the other direction. In a few moments, I would be captured.

It was sooner than that. Before I could even finish my thought, I was grabbed from behind and pulled out of sight. A hand was over my mouth. I thought about biting it, but decided against it. For now. I waited and watched as the Martian patrols moved past. Then the hand came off my mouth and I was allowed to stand up and take a look at the people who had saved me.

It was the Earth Underground! I was saved at last! I was forever safe!

"Thanks, fellas," I said. "You saved my life. Now I'd like to do something for you. Uh... how does eight dollars sound?"

One of the Earthmen looked closer at my face.

"Well well well. If it isn't General Burly of the Martian Army."

"Hello!" I said.

Their unfriendly faces seemed even more unfriendly now.

"I was looking for you guys," I said, a little uneasily.

"That's a coincidence."

An officer of some kind stepped forward. "Remember me, General? You kicked me in the ass."

"I kick a lot of people." I looked at his ass. "Oh, yeah, hi."

This is when I discovered that I had escaped one group of pursuers only to be captured by another. The Earth Underground had been looking for me too. They blamed me for the loss of their planet. And they were planning on taking it out of my hide.

I broke free and tried out-running them, but they were all in better shape than I was, so they caught up with me pretty quick, and began running along with me. They weren't angry. This was the way they were taking me anyway. We were almost there now, thanks to my running. I didn't try that again.

Suddenly we stopped and ducked into the shadows. A Martian patrol was up ahead, looking for me in a row of garbage cans.

"I'm over here!" I yelled. "Help! Help! Hilfen!"

Before I could say any more, the Earthmen dragged me out of sight.

CHAPTER FOURTEEN

The Earth patrol that had captured me cautiously wound its way through the streets. It took awhile to get to where we were going, because we had to avoid Martian patrols as we went, and occasionally had to stop at drugstores to see if we could find anything to keep me quiet.

We were nearly discovered by the Martians at one point. We had to quickly duck into an alley and everybody pretended they were kissing me. The lead man in the Martian patrol shined a flashlight on us, grimaced, then moved on. We stopped kissing, everyone did a lot of spitting, then we continued on our way.

Finally we got to an old 3-storey brick building that was not quite as solid as it looked. Four of our men pushed the building to one side, revealing a hole. We went down this hole and after a moment the building slid back into place. Pretty slick, I thought.

As we worked our way through a maze-like series of underground passages, we passed lookouts who were posted along the way. Each looked us over, then lowered their guns when they saw who we were.

Finally we reached the Earth Underground Command Post. I was roughly shoved inside. Unfriendly faces turned to look at me.

"Here he is, Major."

"Ah, General Burly."

"Hiya."

I looked around. The room was dirt, shored up by planks. The walls were covered with maps, including a map of the Underground leaders' homes, as well as a chart showing the Earth Command leadership from top to bottom. That might come in handy, I thought.

"Hey, can I have that?" I asked the Major, pointing at the chart.

"No. I'm not even sure why we have a chart like that."

A small man in the back of the group spoke up. "Hey, I like making charts, okay?"

"Okay, okay. It's just that... oh never mind."

"Charts are useful. I mean, what if we forgot which one of us was boss? Or who was third least important? The chart would tell us. We wouldn't have to guess."

"Okay, that's enough about charts."

"For now."

"Yes, all right, for now."

Also on the wall were wanted posters for "Frank the Terrible" and "Burly the Beast". I hoped these posters weren't referring to me. I hoped they were referring to some other Burly the Beast.

The Major – Major Zedo his name was – began to read off a list of the atrocities I was supposed to have committed. As I listened, I became more and more outraged. These were terrible things I was being accused of!

"I never did that, I swear to God," I protested.

They showed me a picture of me doing it. "Oh that," I said. "Yeah, I did that." I looked at more pictures. "And that... and that... shit, I did all this stuff." I looked at the pictures again, then pointed to one of them. "Can I get an 8X10 of this one? The one of me kicking you?"

"No 8X10s."

"Oh. Okay. Look, I'm sorry about all of this, deeply and truly and honestly sorry, but..."

"Sorry isn't good enough, Mr. Burly."

"What!"

"You heard us."

"Well sorry is going to have to be good enough, because sorry is all I've got." I made one last attempt to placate them. "Okay, I'm sorry and five bucks."

"Still not enough."

"Hey, screw you, buddy. That's a good offer."

The Earthmen grumbled angrily. I tried to reason with them.

"Okay, listen up. Okay, it's true I'm one of the Martians who invaded your puny planet." There was louder grumbling at this. "Wait wait wait, hear me out. Yes, I am a Martian General, and I have beaten and killed some – underline 'some' – of you. But, and this is important..." I stopped. I'd forgotten what I was going to say.

My audience was getting restless. Then I remembered where I was going with this. "But, I'm an Earthman just like you. I was born here just like you. The only difference between you and me is I fought on the side of the Martians. And we won, too. We slaughtered you guys." I stopped. I'd lost my way again. I decided to finish up quickly. "So the good news is, I've learned my lesson, and there's no need to punish me."

Somebody on my right made a quick move. I grabbed a gun off the table and took a shot at him. That got everybody upset again.

"Would somebody take his gun away, please?"

"General Burly," said the Major, "Whether you did all the things you are accused of is unimportant. Where you were born is unimportant. You conquered our planet. That is the one thing we cannot forgive."

"I took over the planet so nobody else would get it," I assured them. "You guys should be thanking me instead of yelling at me. I can't believe you're so stupid. You Earth People and your stupid minds! Oh Man! Man!"

"Watch your step, buddy," said one of the Earthmen.

"All right, I'll watch my step, but remember what I said about your minds being stupid."

They said they would remember.

"Besides," I said, trying to win them back again. "I have a plan for getting you your planet back. That's what I've been trying to tell you, if you would only listen."

"Okay," said the Major. "Let's hear your plan."

"What... now?"

"Yes, now."

"Uh..."

I had to think of a plan quick.

"Are you asleep, General?"

"What? No, of course I'm not asleep. What's the last thing anybody said?"

"Your plan. We're waiting to hear it."

I tried to think. Suddenly I remembered something I'd seen once in the movies.

"My plan is that we should mobilize our giant spiders..."

"We don't have any giant spiders."

"Well, crap..."

I started to suggest we attack the Martians with our zombies, the zombies could ride our runaway robots, but they said they'd heard quite enough from me. They told me my trial would have to wait, because they had something big brewing, but as soon as it was successfully completed, I would be tried and executed.

I was unhappy to hear this. "Not another trial!"

"Silence! Take him away and teach him to have some respect for the Underground."

"I think you'll find it's hard to teach me anything."

They took me away and locked me up for awhile, but my trombone imitations annoyed my jailors and eventually they turned me loose to roam around in their underground city until it was time for my trial. They didn't have to worry about me escaping. They knew I could never find my way back to the surface. They had picked up the trail of crumbs I had dropped.

The underground city that had grown up around the simple command post was very impressive. Thanks to frequent surface raids, they had been able to duplicate life on the surface to a surprising degree. They had stores, roads, night clubs, even a slum area for underground people who weren't doing so good.

A lot of the people down there had developed large luminous eyes. I complimented one of them on the fast evolution job he'd done. "I'll bet Charles Darwin is looking down from Heaven and is really pissed," I told him.

Since I hadn't been underground long enough to develop luminous eyes, I was issued a pair of flashlight glasses – to aid in seeing underground. I put them on backwards the first time, but that's the kind of mistake you only make once or twice. Once I had them on right, I wondered how I'd gotten along all these years without eyes like oncoming freight trains.

"Can I keep these?" I asked the flashlight glasses guy.

"You can use them. They are yours to use."

"I know that. But what I'm wondering is, can I keep them when I no longer have any use for them? Can I sell them and keep all the money? Are they 'mine' in that sense?"

"No. All flashlight glasses belong to the Revolutionary Underground. They must be returned to the Revolutionary Underground Flashlight Glasses Guy when you're finished with them."

I was disappointed. I could have used the money I would have gotten for those glasses. I was in for other disappointments that day. They wouldn't let me sell any of their stuff.

Besides the big eyes, the main thing you noticed about these people was that they wore plenty of thick makeup to make themselves look more "human". They had gotten too pasty faced and weird looking after living underground for so long. But the makeup just made them look more grotesque. Sometimes this made them so mad they felt like they just had to eat everybody.

For some reason, along with their deformities came an unaccountable feeling of superiority. I wouldn't have felt superior if I looked like that. But they did. They told me they were thinking of destroying all human specimens who weren't as perfect as they were. They said they had had a lot of time to think down here, and this is what they'd come up with.

"You call that nose perfect?" I asked, pointing.

"Yes. And I'll thank you not to bring up that example again."

I was pretty much left alone to wander around wherever I wanted. Nobody bothered me much. Occasionally some of the residents recognized me as being Burly the Beast and started to set off a big stink about it. But after I assured them that everyone knew it was me and that they were in fact the last ones to find out about it, they slunk away, disappointed.

Even though we were far underground, there was no lack of news from the surface. Couriers were constantly moving back and forth between the resistance fighters above ground and the ones below. One of the reports that came down from the surface mentioned that there were Martian patrols everywhere looking desperately for me.

I didn't have any idea why they were so anxious to find me. I was an escaped prisoner, but there were lots of those now that everybody had learned the garbage truck trick. There had to be another reason. Maybe the Martians were sorry for the way they had treated me. Maybe they wanted to apologize and give me back my rank and privileges. This train of thought led to the idea that maybe they wanted to fight another war with somebody and needed good old General Burly to lead the way. I decided that this must be it.

I wrote a letter telling the Martians where I was, and bribed a guy to take it topside and put it in a mailbox. He wanted five dollars to do this, but I convinced him a dollar was all he was going to get.

An hour later I was in the Command Post, standing in front of Major Zedo and the rest of the Underground leaders. Without preamble, the Major began reading my letter aloud.

In this letter I said I'd managed to infiltrate the horseshit Earth Underground and had a list of their physically unattractive leaders which I would gladly trade for the Martians rescuing me and dropping all the criminal charges they had against me. None of this went over very well, as you can imagine. The words "physically unattractive" bothered them the most. I saw a few of them glancing in a mirror and frowning.

I said they had read my letter out of context. You can't get mad at me on the basis of one isolated incriminating letter. I'm a more complex man than that. You've got to get mad at the whole Frank Burly. Don't you see that?

They said they were mad at the whole Frank Burly. So mad they could spit. And they were going to execute me as soon as their meeting was over.

"What about my trial?"

"You've had your trial."

"How did I do?"

"You lost."

Ignoring my protests, and my demands to see a transcript of this trial, they handcuffed me and sat me down in a corner out of the way. While I sulked, they went on with their meeting.

They were making their final plans for the big counterattack. They were going to try to re-take the Earth. A few problems still needed to be ironed out before they could try it though. They still didn't have the secret access codes to the gate at the military base, for example.

"Oh, I know those," I said, bored.

"Silence!"

They also still needed a way to open the special locks at the defense headquarters.

I yawned. "My retina scans will work on those locks. I used to go in and out of there all the time."

"Somebody gag that guy!"

"Wait!"

Major Zedo came over and, one by one, laid out all their remaining problems. I was the answer to all of them.

"Oh, sure, I know where that is... yeah, that guard is a buddy of mine... that's no problem, that alarm doesn't work. I installed it."

"Can you operate a Martian saucer?" Major Zedo asked breathlessly.

I was still feeling pretty sulky – I don't like being executed. I don't care whether it's justified or not – but I didn't mind answering that question. I was kind of proud of myself, to be honest. "Hell, I commanded a fleet of those things. I know everything about them. I could probably build you one."

"So that's why the Martians wanted you back so badly."

I blinked. "Why?"

"You know too much."

"Like what?"

"Never mind."

"No, seriously, do I know something?"

They removed my handcuffs and helped me to my feet. They said they'd forget all my past crimes if I helped them pull off this counterattack of theirs. I wondered if maybe they could add some money to their offer, just to sweeten it a little. But they said the Resistance was having a bad year financially so far. So there would be no cash involved in the deal. Finally, I agreed.

Then they let me in on their plan. It had changed significantly since I had become a member of the team. Originally they had intended to break into the Martian Defense Compound, sabotage everything the Martians had to defend themselves with, destroy or disable their flying saucer fleet, then fight the Martians hand to hand until either they won, or, as was more likely, they lost. Now that I was on board, the flying saucers wouldn't have to be destroyed. We could use them ourselves to win back the world from the air.

I said it seemed like kind of a half-assed plan to me. Not nearly as good as the one with the giant spiders, whoever mentioned that. They agreed that their plan was fraught with risks. But they said if it didn't work, they had a backup plan. Plan B, they called it. This plan called for setting off the world's nuclear arsenal and destroying the entire planet. Plan B wouldn't be total victory, but it would be a tie, which is considered pretty good too. I didn't think much of Plan B. Neither did some of the other Earth leaders. But many defended it.

"Better to die free than live in slavery," said one.

"But we'd be dying as slaves, wouldn't we?"

argued another.

"Technically, yes, but we'd be dying as rebellious slaves. Not docile slaves."

"I don't see the difference."

"Hey, now I don't either."

This discussion was cut short by the Major. It was time to move.

We were issued weapons and maps (waste of paper if you ask me), then began our long march to the surface.

As we marched I led the men in an attack song.

"We are the Earth-men, mighty mighty Earth-men!"

"For God's sake be quiet."

"Sing quietly, men," I said.

"Don't sing at all you idiot!"

I nodded and gave the Major the thumbs up. Then I led the men in a hushed cheer.

"Three cheers for our leaders! Hush hush hurrah!"

CHAPTER FIFTEEN

We cautiously emerged from the three-story building that concealed the entrance to the underground. We were led by our chief scout, Scouty. Just our luck, there was a Martian corporal having a smoke right in front of the building. We froze. He turned a light on us. We were all lined up behind Scouty, as still as mice.

"Who goes there?"

"A private citizen out to get a smoke," said Scouty.

This struck the right note.

"It stinks having to come outside every time you want a smoke doesn't it?" asked the Corporal.

"I'm thinking of writing a letter about it," agreed Scouty. "I've already bought the stamp."

They smoked in silence for a moment, each probably thinking what he might write in such a letter. Suddenly the Corporal thought he saw some kind of movement behind Scouty.

"Is there anyone behind you?"

"No."

"Because it looks like there might be someone behind you."

"Of course there isn't. If you don't believe me, see for yourself."

"I believe I will see for myself."

"I insist that you do."

"Oh you do, do you?"

"Yes. Look behind me right now. I demand it."

I was watching all this from the middle of the group. I nudged the man next to me. The guy in the front wasn't playing this right in my opinion. My nudges were ignored.

"If you're using reverse psychology on me," the Corporal warned, "I'm gonna… "

"You're gonna what? What will you do?"

They stared belligerently at each other for a moment, then the Corporal finished his cigarette, stamped it out and turned to go. "I've got to get back to my post right now, but I'll be back."

"You'd better."

He left and our group let out a sigh of relief that had the Corporal back immediately. He looked at Scouty and his unusually long shadow for a long moment, cocked an ear when part of the shadow hiccupped, then abruptly turned and left again, this time for good.

We worked our way towards a rendezvous point deep in the Earth Quarter, where we were met by resistance fighters who had been operating above ground. They showed us the ground transportation they had arranged for us. It was a bus. It was quickly determined that no one in the group knew how to operate a bus. They couldn't even get the doors open. This is where I took over the mission. Without hesitation, I strode forward, hit the button that opened the doors, sat down in the driver's seat and began jingling the fare box. The Earthmen began boarding.

"You have chosen the right man, Zedo," said one member of the group.

"Wait till we get to our objective," advised Zedo, who was famous for his caution.

"No, I'm making my assessment now."

"Very well."

I drove us to the Martian Defense Compound, stopped at the main gate, and hailed the guard.

"Hey, Hank! If you open this gate you can forget the fifty you owe me."

"Deal!"

He swung the gate open and we drove through. It was a good deal for everybody.

I parked the bus near the entrance to the main building. Nobody had challenged us so far, but we still had a long way to go. And as our group piled off the bus I suddenly noticed that we didn't really look like we belonged here. We looked like an army of slaves out for no good. This part of the plan apparently hadn't been thought out too well. I conferred with Major Zedo and the other leaders. We finally agreed on what we would do. Once again, I was the key to the plan.

I put on my feelers (which I always keep in my back pocket to this day – you never know) and started kicking everybody through the front door of the building.

"Come on, let's go, slave scum. Get moving."

We ran into security personnel around every corner as we moved through the building, but since I really was a professional slave-kicker and these really were Earth slaves, our disguises were perfect. I remember I gave Major Zedo a few especially hard kicks, because I remembered some of the things he had said about me before.

Whenever someone challenged us, I told them I was using the slaves to carry these heavy formidable weapons down to that new weapons storage area by the top secret computers. Each time the sentry would nod and say something like: "Carry harder then. Come on, slaveys, carry! Here, you! Pick up that machine gun or I'll whop you good!" I made a mental note to fire all of these sentries if I was ever put in charge of this building.

With the help of my knowledge of security codes, and my all-important retina scans, we were able to surmount every obstacle in our path. Also, my familiarity with the installation itself turned out to be of great value.

"You can just jump over this. Oh, and this thing, don't pay any attention to that. I installed that."

A dangerous moment came when we entered one of the more top secret areas. It was heavily booby-trapped. If they hadn't had me along they never would have made it.

"Now, when you go through this corridor," I said, "disintegrator beams will shoot out of the walls at chest height."

"What do we do?"

"Go down this other corridor. Nobody ever goes down that scary one."

They followed me down a corridor lined with automated snack machines. They all agreed that this corridor was better.

There was a guard at the end of the corridor. I hailed him.

"Hey, Phil, help us with these boxes of dynamite, will you?"

"Sure thing, Frank. Say, I thought they had you kicking slaves."

"I've been promoted. I lead slaves through buildings now."

"Sweet."

Finally we found ourselves deep in the heart of the building where all the most important stuff was – the missile defense system, the planet-wide alarm system, the Hotline to Mars, all the stuff that the Martians needed to defend themselves with. It took about an hour to smash or disable everything.

Then we split up to see if there was anything of importance we had missed. That's why I was alone when I ran into Arthur Gremlin.

We didn't see each other at first. I was in what turned out to be his office, looking over some odd looking coded communiqués. They looked sinister and important, so I spent a few moments trying to figure out whether they should be destroyed or "liberated" (stolen and later sold). What struck me most about them was that they were written in a strange hieroglyphic kind of writing that I had only seen one place before – in the desk Arthur Gremlin used back when he was working for me. I hadn't been able to read the writing then, because I didn't know Martian. I knew Martian now, but I still couldn't read them for some reason.

While I was puzzling over these documents, the Gremlin was in a connecting room behind a glass wall talking to someone over the radiophone. I found out later that he was saying: "I don't care if you're running out of supplies or not. We can't do anything until Burly is located."

Then he turned and saw me looking through his desk.

"He's been located. I'll take care of him. Proceed with the attack."

Then he got up, made sure his gun was loaded, and joined me in his office.

I was making one last attempt to read the communiqués. It had occurred to me that maybe if I held them upside down, closed my eyes, and pretended like I didn't want to know what they said, I'd be able to figure out what they said. As I was trying out this theory I heard a noise that sounded ominously like a cleared throat. I opened my eyes and looked at Arthur

Gremlin. He was pointing a gun at me. He glanced at the paper I was holding.

"So you've guessed," he said.

Well, there's only one answer to that. "Yes," I said. "I've guessed it all." I let him think about that for a minute, then added: "Might as well tell me what I've guessed."

He sighed. "I was afraid this would happen."

"Well it has happened, so get used to it," I said. I sensed I had the upper hand now about something and decided to press home my advantage until I found out what we were talking about. "Nothing in the world can change it now."

"Yes." He started to squeeze the trigger. "Good bye, Mr. Burly."

"Whoa! Wait a minute! Maybe it didn't happen. Better tell me what you think happened before you start shooting people."

He stopped and stared at me a moment, then resumed squeezing the trigger. Fortunately he had one of those movie guns that take about nineteen minutes to go off. I had caught a break there. But I still had to think fast. If I didn't, in less than an hour I would be dead.

"Before you shoot me, will you answer one question for me?"

He nodded. "One question."

"What the hell is this all about? Who are you? What's going on? Why am I being shot? Why won't anyone tell me what's going on? Has the whole world gone crazy? Are you going to just stand there pulling the trigger or are you going to answer me?"

"That's seven questions."

"No, it's one question – a seven parter."

"Very well." He sat down and lit a cigarette. "As you no doubt have already figured out..." he began, and then he went on to explain a whole bunch of stuff I would never have figured out if I'd lived to be a million. For one thing, he wasn't a Martian at all. The little bastard was from Neptune!

CHAPTER SIXTEEN

'Arthur Gremlin' (this was not his real name, he told me, just a cover name) had been sent by the Imperial War Council of Neptune to convince the Martians to attack the Earth. This was a daunting task, because it was well known that no planet in the Solar System was powerful enough to take the Earth, which was estimated at that time to be 40% nuclear weapons. The Neptunians' plan was to get the Martians to attack first, and after they had been obliterated by the Earth's awesome firepower, the Neptunian battle fleet could come in on their tail and essentially attack the Earth before it could reload.

The Neptunians wanted the Earth primarily because of its good location – not too close to the sun, not too far away – and because it's so easy to stand on. You don't sink up to your neck in poison gas all the time.

Disguising himself as a "Country Martian", Gremlin didn't have much trouble getting a high post in the Martian Government. He had a high

IQ, an A-type personality, and was considered the sneakiest little shit on Neptune. And no one suspected he was an alien. None of the Martians believed there were "little, slightly-less-green, men from Neptune." Only children and astronauts believed things like that. But it was difficult convincing them to try to take over the Earth. The Martian motto, which was engraved on some of their early coins was "Well, I dunno..." The Martians thought, quite correctly, that the Earth could beat them pretty easily in a fight, but Gremlin convinced them that most of the Earth weapons were just for show – display pieces made of cardboard and those Styrofoam peanuts people use for packing boxes. And he assured them that the Earth would make an ideal slave colony for the manufacture of the cheap crap Martians like so much. There was money in this, gentlemen, he told them. Big easy money.

It still sounded too risky to the Martians. What if they got hit by some of those Styrofoam peanuts? Those things could raise a welt. The Earth's huge stockpile of weapons still worried them. After all, whatever they were made of, they were still weapons. What finally convinced them to give it a try was when Gremlin said he personally would go down to Earth with a hand-picked group of saboteurs and they would "soften the Earth up" preparatory to the invasion. Posing as magicians (an easy job for a Martian) they would spend their free time infiltrating military installations and defense plants, finding the cracks in the Earth's defenses and creating cracks where there weren't any. By the time the Martian fleet was ready to embark on their invasion, he told them, Earth would be ripe for the plucking.

They finally agreed to this plan, and the Gremlin traveled to Earth to set up a landing field in some cropland outside of Central City which was owned by Neptune. Then he got a job at the bus company, so he could get his agents transported into town after they had landed. Everything was working fine until I happened along.

The Gremlin said he had gotten a job with me so he could find out how much I really knew, and whether I was a danger to the plan or not. When he realized I wasn't a danger, and in fact was quite stupid and a perfect dupe, (I started to interrupt to protest this characterization which I felt was too broad, but then I decided to let it go. It was close enough. Let's hear what else he has to say) he had his agents hire me to infiltrate places they hadn't been able to get into. I could just walk right past "No Magicians" signs, for example.

This worked out quite well for them for awhile. I was saving them time, and causing them no trouble. When I stumbled into one of their meetings they tried to make me forget what I'd seen, but the amnesia wore off and I not only remembered what I had seen, I started trying to tell others about it. So they decided to ship me off to Mars, where I would at least be out of the way.

Some months later, with the attack about to begin, Arthur Gremlin was stunned to read in the Martian Army Gazette that I was to be one of the leaders of the attack. The Council assured him that I was completely brainwashed, probably, but the Gremlin decided he'd better keep an eye on me anyway.

He was even more stunned when my Martian buddies and I defeated the Earth in less than a week. This really threw a monkey wrench into the Neptunian plan. Now the Martians had Earth's arsenal at their disposal to use against any attackers from space. The Neptunian fleet stopped in its tracks and docked on the Earth's two hidden moons – Sneaky and Hidey – to think things over and await developments.

Arthur Gremlin felt all was not lost. He knew the Martians well enough to know that when things were going well for them they not only didn't do anything to rock the boat, they didn't even pay any attention to where the boat was going. He was confident he could count on the Martians to let down their guard.

He was right. The Martians grew lax immediately. They were a Two-Planet People now. Life was good. They kicked back and relaxed. The Neptunian fleet got ready to resume its attack.

But when I escaped and couldn't be found, the Gremlin became worried that I might use my inside information of Martian defenses to help the Earthmen retake the planet. Earth weapons in the hands of pissed off Earthmen were far more dangerous than in the hands of the Martians, who didn't know how most of them worked anyway. So the Gremlin told the fleet to hold its position until I had been found.

Now that he had found me, I could be neutralized and the Earth counter-attack would flounder in its tracks. Then the Neptunians could safely take the Earth away from the decadent and ill-prepared Martians.

I was looking at my watch, wondering how long this explanation was going to take when I realized he had finished and I hadn't heard a lot of it.

"Could you explain that again? I was looking at my watch."

He sighed and explained it again, in a shorthand way, pausing each time I looked at my watch so I wouldn't miss anything this time. Finally he finished.

"I knew it!" I said.

"Oh you did not."

"Well I know it now. That's the important thing. Say, you said 'Arthur Gremlin' wasn't your real name, just a cover identity. What's your real Neptunian name?"

"You couldn't pronounce it."

"Let's hear you pronounce it."

"Johnson."

"John-man," I repeated carefully.

I thought about everything the Gremlin had told me.

"Say," I said, unhappily. "I've got to stop you."

"Too late. Far too late." He resumed pulling the trigger.

I looked for something to throw at the Gremlin, but there wasn't anything close enough for me to grab. So I grabbed the Gremlin and threw him across the room. It was so sudden and uncharacteristic it took us both by surprise. I remember we both yelled "Wow!" His gun skittered away from him, we both dove for it, and that's when our big super-hero fight started.

I had a size advantage, and I was physically much stronger than Arthur Gremlin (or 'John-man'), but he had the advantage mentally.

He used his mental powers to make me think he was a giant monster, or a bomb that was about to explode, or that he was over there reading in the corner instead of right here biting me in the arm. Fortunately, the illusions didn't last as long with me as they would have with anyone else. My brain doesn't retain false information any longer than it retains any other kind of information. He kept thinking he had me now and would start looking for his gun to finish me off. That's when the illusion would fade and I'd be on him again. He'd make me think I was a chicken, for example, but then I'd forget I was a chicken, or I'd start thinking chickens were really tough. It was very frustrating for him.

Finally I managed to neutralize the Gremlin's powerful mind by slamming a desk drawer on it about twenty times. I tied up his limp body and started heading back out to rejoin the others.

As I was locking the door I saw the Gremlin had regained consciousness and had dragged himself over to a transmitter. He was frantically tapping out a message to somebody.

I found out later that he was trying to get out the signal: "Burly at large. Earth forces possible danger again. Abort attack." But at the time I didn't know what he was signaling. I went back into the room and stood next to him as he frantically tapped on the transmitter.

"What's that you're signaling? Stop signaling for a minute. I want to talk to you." He tapped harder. I laughed. "Will you stop?"

Suddenly I realized he must be signaling for his Neptunian friends to attack our planet and come to his rescue. I wasn't going to let him send messages like that.

I tore the signaling device out of the wall and whacked him with it. He fell back and laid on the floor, hissing slightly like a tire going flat. I found his gun, stuck it in my pocket, resisting his mind's insistence that I "fire it. FIRE IT!", locked the door and went to find my Earth buddies.

They had long before finished with their sabotaging and were out looking for me. They asked what had taken so long and I explained that I had had to beat up an old friend. They looked at me, impressed. No wonder I did so well in the Army.

I led them to the hangers where the flying

saucers were kept. The Earthmen shied back a little when they saw them. They are formidable looking machines, especially up close. I told them to come aboard and I'd show them how they worked.

I took them into my flagship, which I was most familiar with, and which still had some of my stuff stored in the locker, and showed them how to operate the controls. It's not too difficult. If you can fly a B-2 Stealth Bomber and drive a dog sled at the same time, I told them, you can fly a flying saucer.

Once I'd given everybody a rudimentary knowledge of how the machine operated, I gave them a few tips on what to watch out for. "This is the lever that sends the engine back to the factory for servicing. Don't pull that. And this button sets fire to your finger. I don't know if it was originally supposed to do that, but that's what it does now."

At this point, alarms were starting to go off all over the base, so I sent the others to their saucers, sat down at the controls of mine, and we fired up our engines.

On the tarmac a Martian General watched us taxi down the runway and smiled. "Wait!" he told his men. "They won't be able to fly them." The troopers watched us until we had flown out of sight, then looked at their still smiling General. "They'll be back," he said.

The Big Battle For The Earth was a bit of an anticlimax, I'm afraid. I'm tempted to put in a bunch of exciting lies here, because I'm sure they would translate into exciting book sales, and I'm probably going to Hell anyway, but I just don't have the imagination for it. The battle was completely one-sided. A walkover. We had the saucers, they didn't. We knew how to use the Earth's stockpile of weapons. They couldn't even find the instruction manuals.

The battle was made even easier for us by the fact that many of the Martians had become so decadent in the months they'd been here, being waited on hand and foot, they had lost the use of their hands and feet, and in a crisis could only wriggle around angrily.

The planet-wide Martian Defense System that I had personally kicked slaves into finishing by my birthday had been put together so perfectly that one well thrown brick could knock the whole thing out. And this brick had been thrown.

Flying saucers in other cities were all either destroyed on the ground or commandeered by Earthmen. Earth had control of the skies almost immediately. After that it was mostly just cleanup. We strafed the Martians' government buildings, leveled their movie star homes, and destroyed their ludicrous "Escape Ladders", which were too short to even reach the Moon, much less Mars. In a surprisingly short amount of time, the Martians were ready to surrender.

I took care of the last bit of armed resistance personally, chasing the fleeing Martian cabinet halfway across Oklahoma, with the King Of The Earth leaning out of the side window of his saucer, firing at me with his ray gun, as he urged the Secretary of State to "step on it". They eventually lost me, but it didn't really matter. The war was over.

I radioed "Mission Accomplished" and started heading back to base. This is when I saw some new saucers of a strange design coming into our atmosphere. I quickly got on the radio. "Nine hundred thousand bogies at twelve o'clock," I said.

There was no doubt of where these new saucers came from. They were all marked "Neptune Royal Air Force" on the sides. While I was radioing this information to base I didn't watch where I was going and when I hung up the radio set and looked out the window I saw that I was attacking the bogies. I was right in the middle of all nine hundred thousand of them.

Panicking in a crisis is one of the things I'm famous for, and that's what I did here. I frantically started pushing every button on the control panel, hoping one of them would make it so none of this had ever happened. But if there was a button like that, I must have missed it. My chair was adjusting itself all over the place and lights were going on and off all over the ship, and I made more coffee than I could ever drink, but I was still surrounded by enemy saucers. It was all still happening. I did, however, manage to hit the rarely pushed "Destroy Own Saucer" button.

Fortunately, I had also pushed the "Eject And Ignite Occupants" button. So I was already floating and burning down to Earth when the saucer blew up, taking two thirds of the Neptunian fleet with it.

The rest of the invaders turned tail and ran. A few of our fighter jets followed them a little ways into space, taunting them, then wished they hadn't done so.

The surviving bogies headed back to Neptune. Our people tapped in on their radio communications and heard that they were radioing "Mission Accomplished" as they flew off. So I guess everybody does that.

As the hero of the day, I was given the honor of accepting the Martians' surrender. Or most of the Martians, anyway. One enterprising Martian negotiated a separate peace and came out of it with eighteen thousand dollars and a piece of New Jersey, but he was the exception. I dictated the terms of the surrender document, but I did such a bad job of it that the Earthmen ended up being even bigger slaves than they were before. This whole agreement was scrapped, I was told to stand slightly off to one side, away from the microphone, and a new surrender deal was worked out. So I guess I'll never make a name for myself as a negotiator.

After the surrender was complete, I contacted The Council back on Mars and told them it was all over. The Martians had been defeated.

"Well, that's good," Frederick said. "because... what!? Wait a minute, who is this?"

"Triple Double General Frank Burly, Resigned."

CHAPTER SEVENTEEN

So that's how it happened that I managed to conquer your planet – not once, but twice. Once as a Martian and once as an Earthman. So I guess I'm a pretty formidable guy no matter what planet I'm from.

Despite my success, I didn't get a whole heck of a lot out of it. The people of Earth presented me with a small citation that said simply "Thanks", with no mention of what I'd done or who I was. It fell off my wall and got dinged up after a couple months so I went down to the dime store and bought another one. It's the thought that counts, cheap people say, and it was plain they thought very little of me.

I was honored in a small way locally. Some of the neighborhood kids wrote "Thank you" on a bag of shit and set fire to it on my doorstep. You're welcome, kids.

After their initial disappointment, the Martians ended up being glad they lost the Earth as a slave labor planet. The six months worth of cheap crap we manufactured for them set their planet back nearly ten years. Standards fell. Quality became a thing of the past. A whole generation of Martians became stupid. "We got out just in time," was their viewpoint on the whole thing. So I guess they won't be trying to conquer us again anytime soon. Just as well, I suppose.

Harvey got his job back, but I guess I didn't tell you about Harvey. Should have mentioned him earlier. Anyway, he's all right now financially. And that leg of his is healing up nice. So we can stop worrying there.

A couple of weeks after the war ended, I found Arthur Gremlin sitting alone in a coffee shop eating a cheese sandwich and a pickle and looking pissed. Now that all the flying saucers were gone, he didn't have a ride back home. Not that a ride back home would have done him much good. There were wanted posters out for him on both Neptune and Mars. Nobody on either planet was very happy with how the war had turned out, and everybody blamed him.

I rehired him as my secretary. Despite his numerous faults, he's still the best secretary I ever had. Nobody answers the phone like he does and he scares my creditors to death. So my secretary problem is solved.

The only problem I have now is that my Martian wife, Blanche, blew into town last week, dragging our yowling kids behind her, and has been looking all over for me saying "Where is that Earth bum?" I've managed to avoid her so far, so maybe she'll give up after awhile and go back home. Let's hope so, anyway. Except for that, things are pretty much the same around here. Which is the story of my life, I guess.